Ever Your Affectionate

Ever Your Affectionate

A PREQUEL TO THE PORTRAIT

MAYA RUSHING WALKER

APOLLO

GRANNUS

Published by Apollo Grannus Books LLC www.apollogrannus.com

Cover design by Streetlight Graphics, www.streetlightgraphics.com

ISBN:978-1-953613-09-7 (ebook) 978-1-953613-10-3 (print)

www.mayarushingwalker.net

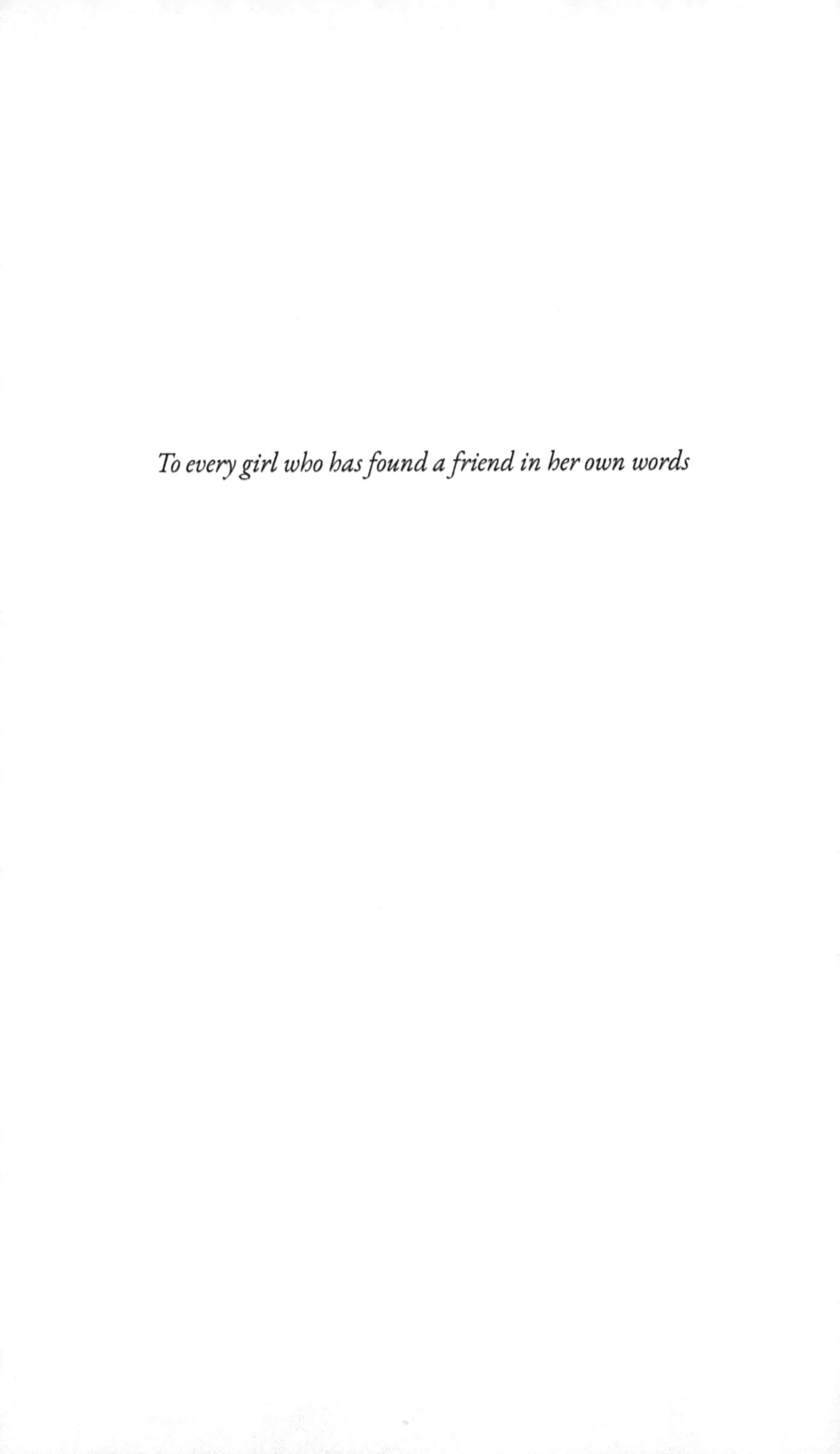

To every girl who has found a friend in her own words

Chapter One

April 1791

My name is Lydia.

My name is Lydia.

My name is

My name is

My name is

(illegible blob)

This pen writes very ill indeed.

Or perhaps it is I who writes very ill indeed.

Ha.

(more blobs)

Must. Keep. Trying.

(series of fancy curlicues)

I've mended the pen. Again. It is a bit better now.

It was my birthday, and Papa gave me this pocket book. I had no pen, but Marianne gave me one. Louisa did not like that he gave me a gift, as she would rather pretend me away. She tried to say something rude, but Marianne hushed her.

I am nineteen years old today.

I have never had a book like this. It has many thin pages in a fine leather cover. I am ever so pleased. Marianne has many, and when she saw how delighted I was, she whispered that she would give me some of her unused pocket books. She did not know that I would like writing in them, as I was always an indifferent student.

Louisa, of course, had to outdo Marianne and say that she would give me her unused books as well, since she is older and about to have her Season.

I don't care who gives me pocket books.

I am over the moon.

I heard Lady Durand talking to Louisa because Louisa was cross about Papa giving me the book. She told her that I was to be sent away because it was awkward to have me around during Louisa's coming-out year. I don't know why it should be awkward. I am not pretty (although neither is Louisa). No one will notice me. But I must go where I am told.

Lady Durand is not mean to me, but she does not like me. Who can blame her, since I am not her daughter? She is obsessed with preparing for Louisa's first Season, and I expect she would like me to just disappear so that I don't raise questions or cause shame.

Marianne is nicer to me than Louisa is. But she is younger. Perhaps she will become mean when she is older. Louisa was once kind, but she has not been nice to me ever since Master Howard said that she was a stupid girl and that it would be better if she were the illegitimate child instead of me—

Blast! I must go now. I hear someone calling for me. If anyone were to find this book…well, I think Master Howard would laugh at me. He might read it out loud to mock me. I would die. But this is where I will record the thoughts I keep in my heart.

You, dear Booke, will always be my friend.

And I will be ever your most affectionate Lydia

P.S. Master Howard told Louisa that I would take precedence because I was older. He was joking, but Louisa was so horrified she slapped him. That was great fun to see. I wonder if other families have as many slaps as ours?

Chapter Two

Hello, my dear Booke!

You are my only friend! Did I say that before? I have lived here at Rosemont for many years, but we are rather isolated, and I do not know any of the girls in the village. Marianne and Louisa know a few of them, because Lady Durand sometimes calls on people and takes them with her, but she does not take me, of course. I don't mind. Master Howard says all the girls in the village are dull and boring, and while I think Master Howard has many flaws, he is brutally honest and often quite correct when it comes to dull and boring people.

It is strange that I am prevented from being with you only by the absence of pen and ink. I still have the pen from Marianne, but Louisa suggested that I had stolen a pot of ink, and Master Howard said he would search my room. I was frightened, as I did not want him to find you.

I admit I also had items in my room that...yes, I stole them. To clear my conscience, here they are:

- five apples—I keep stealing them because I fear being hungry. (This will not change.)
- needle and thread, which I stole because I fear being scolded by Mrs. Tapworth if there are rips and tears in my dress (why are there so many? This will not change either.)
- a lace handkerchief belonging to my mother, which I stole from Papa's study because I will never see her again. (I would die if Lady Durand were to find this! She would beat me and then she would burn it!)
- a dagger Master Howard prizes, which I stole because I hate him and I want him to suffer, since he has never known suffering. (He thinks he has misplaced it and keeps searching high and low for it, ha!)
- a purse of coins I found on the floor of the kitchen after the wine merchant left. (I would have given it to Mrs. Tapworth, but then she would've found out about the wine merchant visiting Mrs. Hobson so often in the kitchen, and there were too many terrible consequences to imagine, so I stayed silent. Mrs. Hobson is kind to me and treats me as if I'm just the same as Marianne and Louisa, which we know I am not, and if she is sacked, I will have one fewer person to help me avoid Lady Durand's wrath the next time I am caught with a meat pie.)

There are other things as well, but those are the ones that I worry will get me into the kind of trouble that cannot be fixed. There are two kinds of trouble—the kind that can be fixed, and the kind that cannot be fixed—and I know them both well.

I also have a knack for finding lost items. I think of a lost item as a piece of a puzzle. And when I hold the missing piece of a puzzle, it feels as if I am the answer to the question.

What question? Well, I don't know, of course! But I enjoy the feeling that I am what others need, even when they do not realize it.

So long as I can find a pen and ink, I can tell you these things. Incidentally, I did not steal the pot of ink—I only borrowed it, and I put it back when I was done. It lives on the writing table in the library, and no one goes in there anyway.

I do not believe Louisa has picked up a pen in years. Marianne wouldn't care if I had indeed stolen a pot of ink, as she is fond of drawing and has many pots of ink. Master Howard is the one I fear most. If Louisa has put it into his head that I am a thief, he may start to watch me more closely, and then he will see that I really am a thief.

But I know you would never betray me! I will always be your protector as well.

I am always yours truly, ever your most darling, affectionate Lydia

Chapter Three

Good morning!

I am sitting under a tree in the far apple orchard. No one comes out here because the trees are so ancient and gnarled. The apples aren't very good, filled with worms and dents. I wonder how old these trees are, and I wonder why no one takes care of them. It seems very strange to ignore an entire community of living beings. When I see them from afar, they look like people. Old people who have lived lives, not young thoughtless people.

Yesterday Lady Durand told me that I was a pert, insolent girl. She charged up to me as if she wanted to kill me, but all she did was slap me hard across the face. Master Howard said later that there was a handprint on my cheek. Lady Durand has very good aim. I've slapped Master Howard many times and have never achieved a perfect handprint. I usually don't get him full across the face and end up hitting the edge of his nose or his jaw, and then he laughs at me.

Maybe it was not so much Lady Durand's aim but that I did not wish to break my stare. Perhaps that was indeed insolent of me, but is not breaking your stare a sign of guilt? I can tell when Louisa lies to me because her eyes grow shifty and she tries to appear casual.

I think I am as pert and insolent as Lady Durand says.

Sometimes I feel bad that she must look after me. My existence is not her fault. She has tried to raise me properly, but she does not like me. And it is not because I am the child of her husband's mistress. She does not like me because I am not nice.

Marianne is nice. She is good-hearted and innocent. Sometimes, when she gazes at me with her big brown cow eyes, waiting for me to explain myself when I have already finished speaking and am on to my next thought, I wonder if she is stupid.

Then I wonder...does she know who I am?

Does she understand that her father was with a woman other than her mother?

Does she know where babies come from?

And of course, that is all rubbish. She has seen the dogs and cats in the courtyard; she knows how babies are made. She knows that her mother is not my mother.

She does not remember a time when I was not here, so she treats me with affection and courtesy, but her mother makes it plain that I am not like her.

I do not think she is stupid. But I perplex her.

And Louisa—she does remember when I was not here, although perhaps just barely, as I arrived here at Rosemont when I was four and she was three. This is why she hates me so much, I believe. She was perfectly friendly to me when we were children, but at some point after Master Howard pointed out that despite my situation I was smarter than she was, she decided that my arrival was the source of everything wrong in her world.

She stayed in the schoolroom longer than she need have because Lady Durand wants her to marry well. She is not pretty, and the past two years there have been several beautiful dark-haired heiresses presented in London, so Lady Durand knew it would be difficult for Louisa to be noticed.

I think it's all idiotic. First, Louisa is the daughter of a duke. Does that count for nothing? I assume she will have a sizable portion, and because she has been hiding away out here in the country, no one knows of her. She will be sought after just because of her fortune, I imagine.

Second, Louisa need not worry about dark-haired heiresses. She presents no competition in the beauty department regardless of hair color. She has a mean, grim face. I think her anxiety makes her even uglier than she is. And weighing her down with diamonds will only make it worse. She needs to find a sharp, interesting fellow who isn't afraid of her cutting way of speaking.

You would think Lady Durand would ask my advice, since I am so wise about these things! Ha.

I will not speak of Master Howard today, as I cannot bear to even write his name. Horrible creature.

You wish to know if I am to be out at the same time since I am so close to Louisa in age? Well you may ask, my dear Booke. I am not to have a Season. And I am going to be in trouble for shirking my chores this morning, so I will not explain why now. But life is hard when you are a child who should not exist.

If not for me, these written words would not exist! So I know that you love me, because without me you would have no life, no thoughts, no language. And in exchange, I love you, because you hold proof that I do exist and have existed.

Which is why I will always, always remain very affectionately yours ever after,

Lydia

Chapter Four

My dear Booke,

I talk to you in my head all the time. Is this a sign that I am not in my right mind?

I think not, although I have very dark thoughts sometimes, and I wonder if this is normal. Do others have dark thoughts on occasion?

Here is my list of dark thoughts:

...

Hmm. Perhaps I should not write them down. What if someone finds you?

I have taken the trouble to bring my pot of ink to this far corner of the storage room. It has a stone floor, which is quite uncomfortable, but I can be sure not to get ink on myself by setting the inkpot on the floor next to me. Yes, yes, you have caught me—I have stolen a pot of ink, just as Louisa suspected. I'm sorry I did not admit this earlier. I suppose I prefer not to think of myself as a thief, but if I did not gather items around me myself, I would be left to build my world out of the items that were thrust upon me. And then I would be the creation of others.

Of course, we are all created by others. I am supposed to believe that God created me, but that is not true. That is a story fed to us at church to keep us humble. Who can stand up to God, after all? In truth, my flesh and bones were created by an act of fornication by a duke and his mistress. That is a fact.

My mind, however, is my own, if I choose to free myself from the influences around me. Even if my flesh was made by the duke and his mistress, I control my spirit.

See, this is why Lady Durand says I am pert and insolent. It is because I am pert and insolent.

I think my thoughts and feel obliged to no one.

My papa keeps me here with his real family because my mama threatened to end her life. She was insane, you see. I once heard someone telling a new housemaid the story of how I arrived at Rosemont, how I was found wandering up and down the road in my nightgown back in the village where I was born, and all the while Mama screamed and wept in her bedroom and tried to jump out the window. It sounded very dramatic, like the entire village was in an uproar. In the end, Lady Durand herself begged Papa to bring me here because she feared the scandal it would cause if my mama ended her life and the blame was cast on Papa. I think that was only part of her fear, however. I think she was also worried that I might pop up someday in the future and shame Papa.

Now that I think of it, it was brave of Lady Durand to do this. It was self-serving as well, of course. But Lady Durand has courage.

That leads me back to my dark thoughts.

The first one is that I hate cowards. This is why I do not really mind Lady Durand but I dislike Louisa so much. Underneath her nastiness, she is a coward. I believe nastiness is often a cover for cowardice. What bad thing could possibly befall a young lady whose father is a duke? There is no excuse for cowardice in her situation.

Is there ever an excuse for cowardice? I do not believe so. I suppose if you were about to hang, I would excuse cowardice in facing the rope. But mostly not.

Why is this a dark thought? Because I feel no compassion for cowards. In fact, I feel very little compassion for anyone. Marianne, who is a good person, feels compassion for the mice her cat brings to her. Not me. Compassion is a useless feeling. No one feels compassion for me, so why should I indulge in such a weak emotion?

Lady Durand feels no compassion for me. And other than giving me this journal, Papa does not think of me one way or the other. Compassion does not help me, and I do not believe it helps others. Only actual acts of generosity are worth anything. Compassion is an excuse to do nothing and feel smugly virtuous.

Another dark thought is that I wish Master Howard would die. Because then the dukedom will pass to some cousin or other, which would serve Papa right for the suffering he has caused.

I dislike Master Howard. I believe I said so earlier? He seems to like me, because he teases me and is not cruel like Louisa. I dislike him because he is a boy and the world is unfair to girls. He was nearly a year old when I was born and nearly five when I was brought to this house to live. I suppose he feels like he is my brother.

He has told Marianne that I am the only smart girl he knows. Such arrogance. I daresay he said this just to make Marianne upset. I told her that he is one of the dumber boys I know, but that was a lie. I said it because he annoys me, but in truth I do know smart men. I shall make a list of smart men. It's quite short.

- Roger, the groom
- Peter, the groom's boy
- Jonas, the underbutler
- Papa's man of business, Mr. Humphrey

And if I have to be honest—with you I am trying to be honest!—Master Howard.

All the other men I know are dumb.

You wonder why Papa is not on this list? I wonder as well. He seems like a thoughtful person, but I keep thinking of Mama and what a dumb thing he did by taking up with her. So I can't really include him.

I'll eventually tell you about the others on the list.

Master Howard is not as smart as the other men on the list, so I feel he doesn't belong there. But honesty compels me to put him at the end, almost as a side thought. (Side thought? Is there such a thing? In my head there is!)

A smart man knows how to do useful things. Master Howard may be clever, but he cannot do anything useful. Jonas once fixed a vase I chipped by knocking it against the wall when I picked it up to examine it. He did it so that no one could see the chip. The vase cost as much as one of Papa's horses, he told me! (I do not understand why Papa spends that much money on horses he never rides.)

A smart man also recognizes the many smart women who make the world work. There aren't many of these men, which is another reason my list is so short.

I have many dark thoughts, and I've only named two of them. Here's my deepest, darkest thought: One day I will leave this place, and I will never look back. I will never be under the control of Master Howard, which is what will happen when Papa dies. I will never be under the control of a husband.

I will take care of myself. But you will come with me.

And I will be ever your affectionate Lydia

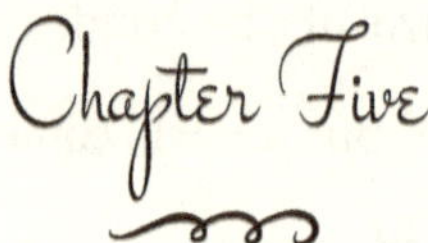

Chapter Five

Summer feels very long this year.

All is in a flurry as the household prepares for Louisa's Season. Marianne keeps pulling me over to gasp over the dresses.

I am not interested.

I am older than Louisa by a year, but I have not had a Season, and I will not have a Season. I promised to explain, and I am determined not to lie to you. So here it is.

My name is Lesley Lydia Barrow. Yes, Barrow as in barrow, the thing you roll about the yard, gathering sticks or branches or brush. The duke's name is not Barrow, of course. His name is Leslie Charles Buckingham Durand, and he is the third duke of Leicester.

The story about my name is thus. I am the natural daughter of the duke, but when my mother discovered that she was with child, she persuaded a man from her village to claim the child as his. The man was a builder named Jonathan Barrow, and when my mother's condition became known, she went to live with him. But he is not my father.

My mother, as I have said, eventually tried to take her own life out of despair and no small amount of insanity, and Lady Durand—for Papa keeps no secrets from her—insisted that I be brought here. She feared what might happen if my mother were to succeed in killing herself and the duke's child were to be brought up by a man such as Jonathan Barrow. This is what I have heard.

When I was little, people did not hesitate to speak in front of me because they thought I did not understand, but I have an excellent memory, and I often pondered these things at length. As I got older, people stopped speaking of these matters in front of me, but just as I am able to find lost items, I am able to pick up lost pieces of information quite easily.

It's a talent, I'm telling you.

I often try to understand why Lady Durand did what she did. What exactly did she fear, I wonder? That I would be vulgar and crass? Would it have been better for me to have been brought up by my mother, who by all accounts was not right in her head? If you ask me, Jonathan Barrow was probably the less concerning choice to parent a child.

But let me finish my story.

The duke had taken up with my mother, the daughter of an itinerant artist, because she was a great beauty and a talented artist herself. She painted miniatures that captured his fancy, according to the story I heard whispered by Bettina the chambermaid. Isn't that a perfectly lovely tale? It sounds like the ideal setup for a tragic love story.

Sometimes I wonder if he ever thinks about my mama. Was he madly in love with her, or only a little? Was it her art that captivated him? He does not seem heartbroken over never seeing her again. And he does not pay much attention to me, but he does not pay much attention to his children by Lady Durand, either.

I am not beautiful, unfortunately. I take after Papa, which would be very funny if it weren't so distressing to everyone who meets me. We have the same hair and eyes, the same forehead and nose, the same mouth and chin. We even have the same build.

Louisa is very clearly my sister, as she has the same strong features, though she is not as tall as I am. Marianne looks like Lady Durand, so she has delicate features, though she has the same dark hair as Louisa and me.

Do not ask about Master Howard—he pulled out my knitting stitches this morning, and I very nearly caught him when I chased him down the stairs. Mrs. Tapworth grabbed my arm as I ran past and gave me a terrible scolding. I do not know how a near-grown man like Master Howard can continue to be such a brat.

But back to what I was writing...

I am not to be called Lesley anymore, as I was named after Papa, and this upset Lady Durand greatly. She thought it was impudent of my mother to name me after him, although this causes me confusion, as my surname is legally Barrow. I was baptized Lesley Lydia Barrow, and why should my Christian name not be shared by others? Louisa was named after Papa's sister, and there are Louisas everywhere, even in the kitchen and the cottages beyond the lane.

Lady Durand is deathly afraid of scandal. I know I have said that she is not a coward, so in this instance I must concede that perhaps I know little of the world, but I simply do not understand why it matters what I am named.

That, dear Booke, is why I will not have a coming out or a Season and why I will not attend any of Louisa's balls or be presented at court. I am the girl Lady Durand has taken in as an act of supposed charity, though I know she was not really thinking of my welfare, just of her own pride and the reputation of the family.

While I am sure that the household has guessed that I am Papa's natural child, as far as I can tell there has been no scandal. Everyone appears willing not to talk about the improper liaison Papa engaged in nearly twenty years ago. So long as I do not disturb the peace, it seems that Lady Durand made the right decision.

My future, you ask? I suppose I will be here until Lady Durand has disposed of the girls by finding them husbands. Then perhaps a husband will be found for me, I suppose. But I intend to be gone long before that happens.

Chapter Six

My dear Booke,

You were surely astonished to find yourself bouncing around in a trunk, buried in clothes, and not seeing daylight for many days. I am no longer at home with the Durands, for just as Lady Durand said to Louisa, I have been sent away.

Being that you are the nearest thing to my heart, you are probably wondering how I feel about being sent away like this.

I do not know how to reply.

Perhaps my heart has coarsened, but I am not sure I feel much of anything.

There are things I miss about home, such as the old apple orchard, but I think I am not a country girl at heart. I am near the city of Bath now, and I much prefer it. I have more freedom to come and go, and there is much more to see and do.

But I am so sorry I have not written to you for a long time. There have been many complications, but I will tell you all.

Louisa is in London with her mama, but I am not at all sure that her Season is going well. Lady Durand did not want to present her when other young beauties would be competing for the attentions of the marriageable young men at the balls and parties. London society reminds me of the county fair, with its prizes for largest turnip and fattest sow! It is nothing but a marketplace, and it is revolting. But back to my point, which is that apparently there are several beautiful heiresses present this season, which means Lady Durand did Louisa no favors by holding her back these past two years.

Louisa's recent letters to Marianne sound furious. I am laughing, but I suppose it's not really funny, since it involves her future. I just find a wry amusement in Lady Durand's attempt to wrest control of Louisa's fate from the hand of...well, fate, or God, or who knows whom.

Master Howard has gone down to Oxford. Before he left, he came to me and tried to say something, but I would not have it, so we quarreled and he left. I was glad. I was beginning to think that he had been in my room, searching for you, perhaps. Several times he came upon me while I was writing, and he kept asking what I was writing about. He could see that I was writing in a pocket book, but he wanted to tease me, so he accused me of writing letters and said that if I was engaged in a secret liaison, he would tell Papa. I laughed at him then, because Papa wouldn't care, but when he threatened to tell Lady Durand, I became frightened. So many terrible scenarios played out in my head of Lady Durand searching my room for love letters and finding YOU instead.

I did not want Master Howard to know that he had this power over me, so to distract him I threatened to tell Lady Durand that he had once stolen an ugly but valuable tiara from her jewel case and persuaded one of his horrible Oxford friends to dress up in ladies' clothes with the tiara on his head. (Of course, at the end of their stupid drunken party he could not find the thing, so he was forced to ask me for help—I am the queen of finding lost items, remember—and I did find it caught on a tassel behind the heavy draperies, which really makes me wonder what on earth these Oxford boys are supposed to be learning at university.) He became very angry and said something about us being allies, which I thought was quite dumb—he is the viscount and the future duke, so how can he be my ally?

Stupid. I hate stupid people. Well, Master Howard is not stupid, but sometimes he says irritatingly stupid things.

So this is what happened. Louisa was sobbing and saying she was afraid of London and would miss us, which of course I did not believe for one second. Marianne was weeping, so I think Louisa felt she had to weep as well. There is not an ounce of sincerity in Louisa, and she copies Marianne when she wants to pretend to be sincere. They were carrying on, and while I was watching and trying not to look too disgusted, Lady Durand came to me and said quietly that I was to be sent away to Avoncliff, which is a village near Bath. The family owns a smallish house there, and she said I would be quite comfortable there on my own.

I was quite startled, for I own I had not taken her past threats seriously. I asked her why, and she seemed to grit her teeth before she said that I was not really a member of the family and that I should not interfere with Louisa's future. I must have looked perplexed, because then she snapped at me and said that I should have known I would not be married from her house and that I should be grateful for any kindness she shows me.

This made me very worried indeed. I do not plan to be married at all, but I am not ready to leave. I do not have any money of my own, for what can I possibly expect of Mr. Jonathan Barrow, my legal father? I am sure he does not have anything he can give me. And my mother...she cannot do anything for me. That is yet another story I will tell you one day, but not now. If Lady Durand were to force me out of the house, I would have nowhere to go and no means of supporting myself.

I began to think of all the things I could do. Remember how I said I can find lost objects? That is how I find out Master Howard's secrets, like the missing tiara. If I set my mind to finding a lost object, I will certainly find it. I don't know how I manage to find these missing puzzle pieces, but all I have to do is go to the places where I feel traces of an object's history and walk among them. It is the oddest sensation, that moment right before I spot the missing item.

But this is not something that can make me money. And I will need money to live.

There is only one other thing I am very good at, and that is needle-work. I neither love nor hate it; but I seem to be able to do it neatly and quickly. In fact, when Louisa is kind to me, it is always because she wants me to embroider flowers on her slippers or leaves on her shawl. Even Lady Durand asks me to decorate pillow covers and handkerchiefs for her. I suppose I could earn my way doing needle-work. But is that enough?

These are things I do not have the answers to, and perhaps it is just as well that I have been sent away, as I will be able to better plan my eventual departure. I may take a few things to a shop in town, if I can do so without being noticed, to see what I may get for them. I am afraid that the evil Mrs. Clabbard will hear reports of what I am doing and tell Lady Durand that I am shaming the family by selling things in town, so I have to be discreet.

The duke has apartments right in Bath, but of course that is not where I am. Instead I am in a little country property just outside of the city. Lady Durand means to hide me here so that no one in Louisa's world will see me or ask questions about me when her suitors meet the family or bring their families to be interviewed by the duke.

What I fear, however, is that Lady Durand means to force me into a marriage so that she can keep me far away from the family permanently. If I am married, I become subject to the will of my husband, and I'm certain Lady Durand will give him enough money to guarantee he does her bidding. I wonder if Papa has anything to do with this, or if he even knows? Would marrying me off be acceptable to him?

It is urgent that I find some way to take care of myself so that I do not have to acquiesce to any kind of horrible match Lady Durand might set up for me.

I am comfortable enough here, and I am to have access to a cob that will take me to town whenever I please. Old Mrs. Clabbard, however, concerns me. She is the housekeeper, and I believe she spies on me to assure Lady Durand that I am not up to mischief.

* * *

I wrote the above a few days ago. It has done nothing but rain since then, and because it is fall, it is very dark.

Oh, dear Booke, if you were a person, you would find me pressing my face to you and taking deep breaths, trying to calm myself. Your pages smell like home to me, except that I do not know what home is. Rosemont, where I have spent so many years, is the duke's main estate near Lincoln, where Lady Durand has raised her family...but I am not in that family, and well I know it.

Yes, I admit it. I am afraid. I do not know what is going to happen to me.

I acknowledge that Lady Durand did not create society or its rules. She is subject to pressures she did not invent. Whose fault is it, then, that my life is thus? Even if Lady Durand were the kindest person on earth, there would be no future for me in her family. I will ever be a mistake the duke made. I will ever be the sad result of a love my mother mistakenly thought was real.

One day I will write more about my mother, but not today.

Your leather cover reminds me of the horses at Rosemont and the leatherwork Master Howard once showed me out in the stables. It smells gamey but strong. Solid. This is what I want to be: gamey but strong. Not a lady with fine manners, but a solid person who does not give way under duress.

I once told you that I dislike cowards. But it is a great fear of mine that perhaps I am like Louisa after all—a coward. Will I have the courage to do what I must in order to avoid the inevitable fate that awaits me if I allow Lady Durand to make decisions about my life?

Tomorrow, I will go into town to look at some of the shops where I may sell my needlework. No one knows me, so perhaps I will tell a few lies and see what may come of it.

Chapter Seven

Dearest one,

I have had the most extraordinary day! I will try to tell you all, but I am not really allowed to have this candle, and I am afraid I will be caught. Old Mrs. Clabbard is very stingy. I was tempted to buy some candles today when I went into Bath, but she would claim I stole them from the household stores and make me turn them over, I am sure of it. Horrible woman.

I went into Bath to see if any of the shops might buy my fine needlework. I have several pairs of slippers that I have embroidered over the past year or two, and out of boredom I have developed quite an elaborate pattern of entwined flowers and vines that I repeat in several colors. I have an extraordinary eye for color, if I may say so myself.

It is not so much that my work is complicated as that most girls would not take the trouble to do it. This is something I have learned, that very often it is not a lack of intelligence or skill that gets in the way of success but a lack of patience and willingness to work carefully.

One lucky thing about being a girl no one cares about is that I can roam freely, so long as I am careful to avoid too much notice while I am in town. I see all the fine ladies with their maids and their grooms, and sometimes, as when I went into a tea shop because I was faint with hunger, I get a curious look, as if they are trying to place me somehow.

Am I a lady? Am I a servant? These looks annoy me. *I am a person*, I want to scream! But of course I do not scream, and I try to act in as dignified a manner as possible. Their confusion delights me, but I know that I am playing with fire. One day, if I am not careful, I will get burned.

It makes me dizzy whenever I try to think about what exactly I am supposed to be. So I try not to think about it. But whenever I go into town, I know I cause confusion. If I am a lady, why do I sell my work? If I am a servant, why do I have proper kid gloves and speak as if I am accustomed to ordering people about? Why am I wearing Louisa's old gowns? Why am I out without a maid or a groom? Why, why, why...always why.

I looked at my reflection in the tea shop window as I stood waiting for service. I was wearing an old dress of Louisa's and a new hat. The hat is plain but looks very well on me, trimmed with a feather that Marianne gave me because she could not find a good hat of her own to use it on. Louisa's dress is a dreadful straw color, but it was wet today, so I wore quite a vibrant cape. I know that capes are out of style, but what do I care? Perhaps it made me look dowdy.

In any case, when I went into the shops to ask about selling my needlework, I was treated as a lady's maid, not as a lady. I did not mind...much. Strangely, the shop clerks assumed that I had not done the work myself but was there on behalf of some humble maidservant who worked under me in some great house or other. Very funny! It is strange how the mind will make up elaborate stories to explain something that doesn't fit into a limited model. The story ends up being much stranger than the reality!

The good news is that I can get quite a nice sum for the more intricate needlework. One shop begged me to leave the slippers, so I did. If they sell, then they will ask for more.

My embroidered lawn handkerchiefs will fetch a lot less, but I have some ideas about how I can hem them with an elaborate lace edge. I purchased some supplies, and perhaps over the next week I can experiment with this. I have not seen handkerchiefs of this type anywhere, and the one I made for Marianne has her in raptures every time she looks at it, even though it was a clumsy attempt.

Because it was wet, I decided to take the country road home, as I was slightly worried about footpads. I had spent my money, but I had a few parcels and might have been a target for thieves if I had gone the short way along the open road.

As I was plodding along on a muddy track, I could see clear across the field to where a girl was standing—right in the mud!—and looking distraught. I tried to ignore her, but she had such a horrified look on her face that I called out to her in spite of myself. Then she began to wave frantically. She was up a gentle slope from the dirt track where I had stopped, but my mount went up the rise with no problem, even with the mud.

The girl was a little younger than I, and so beautiful. Golden hair, almost white-blond, and bright blue eyes. She was like a sunflower shining in the middle of this shorn, muddy field.

At first I thought she must be a farmhand or a maidservant, although why she would be in the middle of a field in the rain, I could not fathom. But as I got closer, I could see that her clothes were not those of a servant.

"Please," she said, "please, I need to go home. Will you take me?"

"Where is your home?" I asked.

"Up past the next bend, but you will have to go down the lane, and you will end up at the back entrance. I will show you."

The girl made as if to approach me, but she hesitated, turning around to inspect the grass around her. She seemed distressed, so I looked down and spotted something shining in the grass.

"Is that yours?"

The girl looked up at me, her eyes very wide, and said nothing, so I alighted and fetched the object, which was almost under her feet. It was a locket made of very heavy gold and trimmed with dark red gems. It was old and had lost its luster, but it was unquestionably of value.

I held it up for the girl to see, and her face went white. For a moment, I thought she would faint.

"Are you all right? Are you feeling ill?"

The girl reached out to take the locket from me, her hand trembling, and clasped it to her chest.

"No," she gasped. "But thank you! This is why I am here. I have been searching for this locket for hours. It fell off its chain while I was riding."

"Riding? But..." I looked around. No horse in sight. "Where is your mount?"

Now that I was up close, I could scrutinize her dress. She was not wearing a riding habit. She wore a pelisse in a dark color made even darker by the wet over what looked to be a morning dress in dove gray.

The girl saw my look and flushed with embarrassment. But she lifted her chin and said, "My name is Catherine. I did not ride today. I walked."

Walked? I looked up the slope in amazement. As far as the eye could see, there were wet green fields.

"Will you take me home? I promise I will tell you what happened, but I am afraid of not being home in time for tea." The girl sounded anxious and insistent.

"Of course," I replied. "You will have to just hang on to me as best you can. My mount is gentle, and she will not bolt, but you will have to mind your seat so you do not slide off—"

As I was speaking, Catherine began to walk toward me, and to my astonishment, she had a severe limp. It was ugly, there was no question—she bobbed from side to side—but there was a dignity and pride to the lift of her head, and I realized at that moment that she was someone of great consequence. I could see it in her posture, the way her profile seemed to dare me to comment.

Had she really walked all the way down into this muddy field from her home? Even if it was around the next bend, it was far enough away that I could not see it from where I was standing.

"I am very good with horses," Catherine said. She had reached my mount and was patting the horse's head.

"I can see that." I decided to say nothing of her limp. "Let me hoist you up, and I will take the reins behind you, with my arms about you. Is that all right? Don't worry about this old girl—she's very mild and strong. The gardener's children often ride her two at a time."

Without replying, Catherine turned her back to me and placed her hands on the pommel. I helped lift her up. She was very light, and I was able to heave myself up behind her with no problem.

"You will have to tell me where to go."

Catherine nodded. "Right past the next bend, there is a track that goes downhill. You have probably never noticed it."

"I am new to this area," I confessed.

"It is not far. Not by horse, I mean."

"It must have been a long walk."

There was silence, and then she replied lightly, "I wanted to find that locket, and if I had tried to ride, someone would have made me bring a groom for fear that I would hurt myself. My limp causes everyone to treat me like a child. I ride quite well, but there is no arguing with my jailers."

I almost asked her what she meant by jailers, but an image of Lady Durand came into my mind, and for a moment I was tongue-tied.

Then she laughed.

"You must think me outrageous. I beg your pardon. Take this left here—see, you would have gone right past it and not known it was there. This leads to the back entrance of Wansdyke. It is my late mother's family home. It is rather grand, is it not?"

Just as she said this, I caught sight of the house towering above us beyond the grassy hill and nearly dropped my reins.

Grand was an understatement. Wansdyke was a palace, a spectacular Tudor-era spread that almost eclipsed Rosemont in its level of ostentatious splendor. I gaped at the windows, the shrubbery, the stonework...before I realized we were still moving and that if I did not take care, we would both tumble to the ground.

As we plodded up to the stables, half a dozen stable hands and grooms appeared, ready to take charge of my horse. They all had bland, practiced expressions on their faces, as if they were quite accustomed to their young mistress suddenly appearing on the back of an old cob with an unrecognized companion.

"We must tell them we were together the whole time," Catherine murmured. "They mustn't know that I snuck out alone, or they will watch me even more closely." She raised her voice. "You, there. You will take my friend home in the carriage after we've had our tea. And take care of her mount."

Then, suddenly, she turned. "I don't know your name," she whispered.

"My name is Lydia," I whispered back. "Lydia Barrow."

And now I must stop, dear Booke! I have so much more to say about the tea I had with Catherine and the grand home she lives in, as well as her sad story...but I am very late for my supper, and I am already in trouble with Mrs. Clabbard, for she discovered my stash of embroidery supplies and wants to ask me many questions. She is sure I am a thief, since she knows I did not bring these supplies with me from Rosemont. I hate her!

Chapter Eight

BELOVED FRIEND!

It has been a while since I've written. The days are colder and shorter, and I'm burning more candles to finish a large order of embroidered slippers for another shop in Bath. Someone purchased a pair from the first shop that agreed to carry them, and I believe her sister mistakenly went to another shop to buy a pair for herself. The next time I went to deliver a few things to the first shop, I visited a few others, hoping to find more interest, and discovered that the proprietor of one had already heard of me!

What good fortune!

I also visited the top modiste in Bath, but I am not sure I liked the result. Mme Allard is very busy, and she has a group of women who work for her and do her bidding. I did not like that she wished me to help embroider a pattern of her own design on a court dress. Needlework is relaxing for me so long as I do not feel someone is standing over me with a whip!

I declined her offer of employment with as much dignity as I could muster. It is difficult to be in this humble position of need and to still be dignified, but I do not ever plan to beg for anything, ever, from anyone, ever.

I wrote EVER ever too many times! Ha! I am EVER SO ANNOYING.

I will admit I am relieved that there is work available for me if I get to the point at which I must give up some of my freedoms in order to survive. It would be challenging to make do with what Mme Allard would pay me, but it would be better than being under the control of a man who would treat me like his property while having other women on the side. Disgusting.

I offered to embroider my own designs on Mme Allard's creations, but she snubbed me. In fact, she stared at me as if I were a bug. I was quite upset when I left.

However, now that I think on it, I imagine she was trying in her very French way to figure me out. She has many customers from the very pinnacle of society, and she must be extremely practiced at knowing exactly who is who. I was raised in a duke's home, so I am sure my speech and manners are impeccable...but if I were the real daughter of a duke, I would not be selling my work.

I am a very confusing girl, I admit.

It makes me dizzy to think about what, exactly, I am supposed to be. So I try not to think about it.

I want to tell you more about Catherine, who has been consuming so much of my thoughts as of late. She has reached out to me several times after we took tea together that wet day when I rescued her from the muddy field.

She explained that she had been unable to climb up the hill because of her limp, but she had not understood that this would be the case until she was at the bottom and had turned to try to go home again. She was trying to figure out what to do when I came along the lane quite by chance, much to her relief!

She is a great rider, to my surprise—her leg does not cause any problem for her when she rides. She rides very rough and fast and owns a number of very spirited horses.

That first day, she had me brought back home in her own carriage, which upset Mrs. Clabbard a great deal, ha! Mrs. Clabbard tries very hard to put me in my place and keep me there, but when she saw Catherine's fancy carriage through the window, she ran outside, prepared to scrape and simper at whatever great personage was coming to call...only it turned out to be me! And then she could not speak brusquely to me, as she normally does, because Catherine's coachman was there.

Very amusing!

Catherine also had a groom bring old Molly back, and I learned that he is great friends with our head groom here in Avoncliff. It is a small world.

The following day, she sent me a very pretty note of thanks with a gift of beautiful sweets from a shop in Bath. Oh, I forgot to mention—the locket I found in the grass belonged to her mama, and its chain had broken. I told her I have a magical ability to find lost things, and she laughed so hard! Our meeting was meant to be, she said.

Then she grew serious and confided to me that she has only the one remembrance of her mama, as her papa is stern and cold and got rid of all her mama's personal things when she died.

This took me aback. I did not expect to hear her speak ill of her papa. I don't know that I would be able to say anything bad about Papa to a near stranger. I don't know if I could even say anything bad about Lady Durand, even if it were true! Somehow, it feels wrong to speak openly about one's family like that.

I cannot emphasize enough how pretty Catherine is, so delicate and golden-haired. I am quite struck. I fear I was rude, staring at her the way I did. She has a wonderful trilling laugh, like birdsong. And she often interrupts me with a delightful observation or funny comment, which causes me to lose track of what I was saying entirely.

I enjoyed the tea with her so much; it did not feel like anything I have ever experienced with Marianne, and certainly never with Louisa. And Master Howard doesn't deserve inclusion, since he is a boy, after all, and cannot converse pleasantly with anyone.

In all my years in the remoteness of Rosemont, I have never had a friend. I wonder if I may be so bold as to call Catherine my first friend?

Our relationship is complicated. She is the daughter of an earl, and my papa is a duke, but I am not his legal daughter. So she outranks me, I think?

I am not sure. Certainly I am outranked by Marianne and Louisa, no matter how much Master Howard teases Louisa that I am the elder sister and therefore outrank her. And they outrank Catherine. Bother with these rules of precedence! It is so confusing. These rules do not seem to acknowledge how people really live!

When I reflect on it, my existence is due to a mistake, a liaison that never should've happened between my mama and the duke. And yet, from what I can gather, my mama was madly in love with Papa, so much so that she lost her mind and very nearly took her own life after she had to be with Mr. Barrow. I have never had the feeling that Papa felt the same way about her; after all, great men are always taking up with this or that opera singer or rich widow.

But that is all in my own head. I do not actually know if Papa loved my mama. Lady Durand has never given any indication one way or the other. She certainly feared scandal, but she never appeared to worry about her own position or place in the family.

Would she not have been in a panic if she thought Papa loved someone else? I suppose she need not have worried that he would divorce her, but it was perfectly possible that Papa might have kept company with someone else and paid no attention to his family at Rosemont.

Would that not have been serious injury to her pride, at least?

There is no place for someone like me. I cannot easily keep company with members of society, but I am not a servant, a trades-man, or a common villager or farmer. While I have never minded the thought that I would not have a Season or become the lady of a great house, I cannot say that I am comfortable in the kitchen with the servants, and they are most definitely not comfortable with me. They are not my people.

In addition to the fact that Rosemont is so inconvenient, perhaps this is why I have never had any friends. Marianne and Louisa have cousins, and they have exchanged letters with girls they met on trips to Bath or London. Not me. I have never had anyone to talk to besides my half siblings. No one else knows what to do with me, and I have always been resigned to this fact.

I believe Catherine has detected that my personal situation is confusing, though she has not asked for details, and I have not shared. She immediately told me her story, which quite shocked me, as I am not accustomed to speaking frankly with people outside of Rosemont.

I did not expect that she would be willing to share such intimate details, but she was light-hearted and casual as she explained that her papa was angry that she was lame and not a boy and that he had no heirs. This made sense to me, for this must be a problem for many families. But her stories of how he treats her caused my mouth to hang open with incredulity. It is as if he has ice water in his veins!

Papa has never been that way with me. He is not cruel or vengeful. Catherine's papa sounds as if causing her pain gives him pleasure. Papa has never paid much attention to me, but now I realize that attention can take many forms, and I suppose I have been quite lucky.

Even Lady Durand looks better in this light, for her decision to take me away from Jonathan Barrow meant that I was properly raised. No one has ever been that cruel to me. As you know, I am pert and earn the occasional slap, but that is my own doing.

On the other hand, Catherine tells me these stories with such a calm demeanor, it leads me to wonder if perhaps I am reacting with too much emotion. In any case, she is all but banished to Wansdyke. She has invited me to come and stay with her in the upcoming weeks, and I must admit I look forward to getting away from my own jailer, Mrs. Clabbard!

I earned quite a bit from that first collection of embroidered slippers, but when I decided to start selling my work, I must admit I did not think about the cost of supplies! I ended up spending a great deal on fine threads that I like.

I am also wondering if I can ask someone else to make the slippers for me so that I can concentrate on the design and the embroidery. There is a girl who works in the kitchen who sometimes pauses to look at what I am doing when she passes by. She seems promising. Perhaps she can make the slippers, and I can think about expanding my designs for the kind of dresses Mme Allard the modiste was talking about.

If I had that much space to embroider, I would be very pleased indeed. I will use one of the other pocket books that Marianne and Louisa gave me to sketch my ideas.

Chapter Nine

YOU WILL NEVER BELIEVE where I am writing from, dearest Booke!

I am at Wansdyke, in a wonderful bedroom right next to Catherine's own, with lots and lots of candles. Catherine has seen that I write and draw a great deal, sometimes late into the evening, and there seems to be no shortage of candles in this beautiful place, nor is there a crosspatch housekeeper to remind me that I am but a guest in my own life.

I am bursting with happiness to have a friend!

It is a strange feeling.

She is not like me at all. She is a great outdoorswoman, and as I have mentioned before, I have seen her ride very rough and fast. She took me out shooting with her groom, which I did not know ladies were allowed to do. I put my hands over my ears out of fear of the loud report of the gun, and she laughed at me and said I was very ladylike and should get rid of that "affliction."

I must admit I was dazzled by the thought of a woman who could shoot her own dinner! Can you imagine, dear Booke? Her groom seemed perfectly nonchalant, but he also seemed very paternal toward her; perhaps he has known her since she was a child. Perhaps she learned her skills from him. Perhaps there is much one can do when one's papa despises one's existence.

(This is a new idea for me. Perhaps hatred can mean freedom.)

Catherine does not care if her riding habit gets muddy or her hat gets wet even though she has a beautiful wardrobe, which she admits is one of her weaknesses. She does love fine clothes, but she cannot abide sitting still.

We once got into a mild argument because she wanted me to take her walking and I protested because it was about to rain. She wanted me to go with her because her stuffy dresser insisted that she not walk alone, even on her own grounds, but it was almost time to dress for dinner, so I did not want to get wet.

"You are being a bore," she complained, but with a sparkle in her eye.

"I am saving you from being late to dinner," I countered, "and saving your dress from being spoiled. That lace overdress will snag on the shrubbery."

Catherine *hmph*ed irritably. "We should wear trousers, as the men do."

"How absurd," I laughed. "You know how much you love silk and lace and beautiful hats!"

"I love doing as I please," she retorted. "Don't you? Would you not wear trousers if it meant you would not shred your fine dresses?"

I had to admit she had a point!

I still have not revealed much of myself to her, of which I am rather ashamed, but I know not how to explain my background without embarrassing detail.

Yes, I said embarrassing. I did not feel embarrassed when I wrote everything down for YOU, dear Booke. But I cannot bring myself to tell Catherine about myself, even though I know this is stingy and mean-spirited.

Do I fear she will look at me differently if I tell her my story?

No, she is much too strong to be swayed by the opinion of society. She limps about Wansdyke with a great deal of energy, shouting to her servants and commanding them left and right. They fear and respect her, and they treat me with a deference that I know comes from their opinion of her.

She has asked me where my home is, and I have told her honestly that my papa and stepmama have sent me to Avoncliff to get me out of the way for Louisa's season. She cocked her head at this, but I did not explain why I was a source of trouble for Louisa. That felt like too much detail.

Catherine assumes that Lady Durand dislikes me because she is my stepmama, not because I am illegitimate. That is a common enough thing, I know, and she is being tactful by not trying to pry.

But I think she will soon discover the truth, and then we will see if she is still willing to be my friend. I have no experience with being a social outcast because of my parentage, but I know that in theory I am not fit company for the daughter of an earl.

But she is strong, and I like her. She is honest and kind. She seems to have no regard for what others think about her, so I hope this will also be true for what others think about me. I admire her very much for her courage and honesty.

I have started drawing some sketches of vines and birds in another pocketbook, and Catherine exclaimed over them and asked me what they were for. I almost told her I was selling my fine needlework in Bath shops before I realized this was a bit difficult to explain. Once again, I was in a muddle. Ladies of her rank do not sell things in shops!

So I just told her that I liked to draw and paint designs for needlework. The following day, she took me to one of the several libraries at Wansdyke, where she showed me a desk filled with drawing supplies. I was shocked, as the desk was dusty and seemed not to have been touched in a very long time. She invited me to use the room as I pleased, and I happily accepted. So I have gotten a great deal of work done on my designs these past few days.

I do not look forward to returning Avoncliff. Wansdyke is like a dream to me.

Chapter Ten

Letter from Her Grace the Duchess of Leicester, Lady Amelia Durand

Rosemont, Lincolnshire

To Lydia Barrow, Stonemeadow House, Avoncliff

My dear Lydia,

I write with excellent news. I have managed, with great difficulty and no small amount of expense, to contract a very desirable alliance for you. I am sure you know that it is of paramount importance that your future be settled so dearest Louisa may look forward to her own happiness soon. Louisa has always been so very fond of you, and she insists that the elder should be married before the younger, which is, of course, the proper way to do things.

You have always been a difficult child, but I trust that you see the advantages of a match arranged by myself. This man is decent and willing. Given your circumstances, it is generous of him to agree to marry you, though I have assured him you are not ugly or infirm. I have discussed the details with him, and he agrees that he should call on you in Avoncliff. He is in London at present, which is not impossibly far.

The gentleman's name is Roman Kettering Dryden, and he is the owner of some lands up north in the vicinity of Nottingham as well as some near Sheffield.

Obviously, you must be on your best behavior when he calls. Do not speak or laugh loudly, and do not be rude to him. I do not think he will change his mind, given my assurances, but you will only hurt your chances by behaving as if you have never been taught better. You will embarrass your papa and myself, and I may not be able to contract such a good marriage for you again if this one falls through.

This is all you need to know. He hopes to call on you at your earliest convenience, which is amusing; what can you possibly be so busy doing that a visit from Mr. Dryden would inconvenience you? I told him I would pass his request on to you so that you would not be surprised when he writes.

The duke will be glad to see you married and happily settled in your own establishment in the near future. You do not need to write to thank me, as I am but doing my duty as the mistress of the household. I hope you know that I have always endeavored to faithfully discharge the duty that has been thrust upon me and that I wish you happiness in the years ahead.

AD

Chapter Eleven

Dearest friend,

It is late, and I am very tired. But something has happened, dear Booke. I need to spill this out onto your pages or I will burst.

Lady Durand has sent a letter. She says she has found me a husband and that I shall be married.

I need to run away, and quickly.

I have always sworn that I will not be married. Perhaps this sounds foolish, or even mad. Perhaps I should be afraid of starving or of being alone in the world without a protector. But I am more terrified of being under yet another person's control, this time for my entire life. I am terrified of being told where to go and what to do and how to live. And I am terrified of being taken away from the one person who is my friend.

Catherine has become so important to me. She makes me laugh, and she tells me things that are genuine and true but that would scandalize Marianne and Louisa, I'm sure. For example, she is without emotion when it comes to her papa, and she speaks of him as if he were a servant or a farmhand. She calls him "that man." Once I got over my confusion and discomfort, I realized that she does so because that is exactly who he is to her—a man, someone who has dominance over her merely because of his sex.

He does not treat her like a daughter, and she feels she owes him no respect, so he is nothing but a man. The beautiful Wansdyke estate belonged to her dead mama's family, and this is why she was sent to live there, probably for the remainder of her days. This makes me shudder, but I admire Catherine for refusing to live in a state of self-pity.

She is evidence that the world is not entirely artifice, that something genuine and true exists somewhere. She is so beautiful and yet so strong and imperious. I do not think it is a pity that she has a limp; somehow, her leg makes her look even grander than she would if she were not lame. She does not disappear into the background the way that ladies often do. No, she throws her shoulders back and lifts her head proudly even as she drags her weak leg beside her.

"You, there," she will call out to the nearest footman. "Give me your arm." Servants come running when she begins to thump around a room angrily, complaining about lukewarm tea or dusty cushions.

I once heard her chastise a groom for telling her that her favorite mount was too fresh and excitable for her to take out. "Do not disrespect me!" she warned the poor man. "I am capable of more on a horse than you will ever be, you pathetic creature." And I believe that she really is.

The letter came last week, and for several days I was too shocked even to write to you about it. But then Catherine came to visit, and I showed it to her. She does not often visit me here, but that day she was exercising a nervous mare and traveled farther than she normally would to ride the jitters out of her horse. She called upon me without knowing if I would be home, and fortunately, I was.

I was working on another set of slippers and wondering how much money I would need in order to flee when she was shown into the drawing room.

"Catherine," I burst out when the door shut behind the servant, "I do not know what to do." I almost cried, but I very rarely cry, and I held back the salty feeling in my throat. Instead, I fetched Lady Durand's letter from my room. When I got back, tea had been served, and Catherine was inspecting the shoes I had left scattered about the floor.

"These are lovely," she said, looking up at me. "But why do you need so many pairs of slippers? Are these for cousins at home?"

I was too distressed to lie. "They are to sell in the shops in Bath."

Catherine blinked in amazement. "Sell? Shops? Why?"

"I need to earn money," I said bluntly. "I need to escape my family." When I heard my own words, I could stand it no longer. I began to cry as I handed her the letter, which she quickly opened and read.

I don't remember exactly what transpired next—Catherine folded me in her arms, patted my tearstained cheeks with her handkerchief, sat me down, poured me tea, and then gave me a good shake, I believe! She is not one for tears or sentiment, and I was probably annoying her, especially as she had never seen me show any signs of emotion like this before.

Between sips of tea, I tried to explain my situation, but I kept coughing and blowing my nose. Finally, she shook her head and held up a hand.

"Wait," she commanded. "You are not making sense. Your papa is who, exactly? And who is this Lady Durand? I know she is your stepmama, but this letter …how could she write such a letter to her husband's daughter?"

She shook the letter, holding it between her fingertips as if it were dirty, her pretty mouth frowning in distaste. "It's very rude," she concluded.

At this I hesitated. I do not feel that Rosemont is my home, but it is the only home I know. I could not bring myself to explain that my legal father is Jonathan Barrow of Meadowlark Lane in Gloucestershire, not far from the market town of Stroud.

Life at Rosemont had not prepared me for these questions. Everyone at Rosemont knew who I was. I was struggling just trying to introduce myself in the shops in Bath because I didn't know how to explain myself.

Oh, life is so unfair. At the very least, everyone is supposed to know who he is. I am an inexplicable mistake, a blemish. Certainly there is a logical explanation for my existence, but there is nowhere for me to BE.

THIS is why Lady Durand is marrying me off in this way, I thought bitterly. It is too difficult and potentially too damaging to have me in the public eye in any way. Better to put me under the thumb of some man somewhere who can shut me up in any way he pleases. Most likely, Lady Durand will be only too happy to pay him a large amount to keep me quiet and out of the way of Papa and his children.

When all is said and done, the safest and easiest thing is to conform to societal structures.

Marriage. Money. And men. The three *ms*.

I swallowed another sob, feeling increasingly desperate. "I grew up at Rosemont," I whispered. "I know no other home."

Catherine still looked puzzled, so after I had calmed down further, I said, "Lady Durand is not my mother...and Papa is not my legal father, because he was not married to my mother."

Catherine reached out to clasp my hand but did not look the least bit shocked.

"Where is your mother?"

I shook my head. "I have not seen my mother since Lady Durand moved me to Rosemont. I was very young. I don't remember her at all. I have heard...I have heard that she...she is not well, and her mind was affected by all that transpired after my birth. Lady Durand took me away because my mama threatened to end her life, and I was found wandering about the road with no one looking after me. If I had drowned or come to some other unfortunate end, Lady Durand was terrified that everyone would blame my papa. I was very small when this happened, so I only know what I've heard through gossip."

"Did your papa never acknowledge you?"

I shrugged, sniffling. "Does it matter? My mother found another man to give me his name. Papa did not care one way or the other. I am Lydia Barrow, not Lydia Durand, but I grew up with the other Durand children at Rosemont. I believe my mother saved her own reputation by persuading Jonathan Barrow to claim me, and perhaps she even saved mine! But Lady Durand always does what she can to avoid scandal, and my mother's ravings and efforts to end her life caused so much chaos that she took care of the problem the way she always does—with brute force. And now she will use brute force once more to get rid of me for good because my presence at Rosemont is inconvenient. It has always been inconvenient, but it is worse now that she is trying to see Louisa married. She wants me gone."

"I see." Catherine nodded, and she was silent for a while. Then she spoke.

"You know that Lady Durand cannot force you to do anything against your will. You cannot be married to anyone if you protest."

"Yes. I know that. But I depend on her utterly for my livelihood. That is why I am making slippers." My heart began to race again, and my breath felt stuck inside my chest. "If I do not marry whom she says, I must either find my way in the world myself or find someone else to marry—and I will not! I will not find someone else to own me!"

I gasped this last sentence out, as I felt as if I were being strangled.

"I wish I could take you away from all of it," Catherine said wistfully. "I am not free either. I have nothing of my own. I cannot make any decisions myself. I am a prisoner here at Wansdyke. I will likely never have a Season or marry. It has never really bothered me. What would I want with dancing and stupid people left and right, all of them simpering and scraping? And I am lame, so I cannot travel easily—"

Then she stopped. She cast me a sidelong look.

"I have an idea."

I was not paying close attention at that moment, as I was convinced I was doomed. I was thinking of how many coins I had in my purse, how many slippers I could finish quickly, whether I could possibly find lodging somewhere in Bath if I worked as a dressmaker's assistant.

So I was surprised when Catherine suddenly said in a conversational tone, "I am glad I stopped by today! I was not sure until this minute that I take precedence over you—did you know that I outrank you? I assumed that I did—I outrank nearly everyone—but now I know for sure."

I was so startled that my mouth must have hung open. For a moment, I feared I had just lost my one and only friend. I had always been afraid that if Catherine knew the truth about me, she would no longer want to speak to me. That is what Lady Durand would have said, to be sure.

"But this is good. It suits my scheme nicely," Catherine continued.

I stared, still confused.

Catherine laughed. She patted my hand and stood up with some effort, leaning heavily on me.

"I will come back when I have thought through my scheme," she promised. "Do not do anything rash! We will outthink and outsmart Lady Durand."

Your most affectionate but fearful friend,

L

Chapter Twelve

WHO IS this man whom Lady Durand has found for me to marry?

My dearest Booke, I do not know. She did not say much in her letter except that she would send him to call. This has me in fits of terror. What do I do when he arrives? How can I escape him if he is here in the house?

It has been a week since Catherine was here and I told her all. I have heard nothing from her, and I am beginning to think her calm reassurance that she could help me out of this terrible problem was just her usual calm and not a sign that she has a real solution.

For what can I do but obey Lady Durand? Either I must flee, or I must marry. I am not a legal member of the household. My step-mother is free to turn me out if she wishes. I do not have my father's name or protection. And what can Jonathan Barrow of Meadowlark Lane do for me? Nothing. He neither knows me nor cares about my fate.

I have counted and recounted the coins in my purse, but there is barely enough for the fare to London.

London, you ask?

Yes, London. I know that if I go to London, I can lose myself in the crowd. But I do not have the necessary funds, nor do I have connections who can help.

I have also been thinking that despite Catherine's kind reassurances, I do not want to inconvenience her. She is possessed of a kind heart and a lively intellect, and a friend such as myself will drag her down in the eyes of society. Now that I have finally told her my story, it is clear that she is my better, and she did not hesitate to let me know it.

I have been wondering if I will be invited to Christmas at Rosemont. Will Lady Durand leave me here by myself over the holiday? I have never liked the festivities at Rosemont, but it seems particularly cruel to leave me here alone. There is only a limited staff here, so there isn't anyone who can cook a Christmas dinner or put up greens for the season.

Just listen to me, dear Booke! How can I speak of holiday decorations at such a time, I wonder? I must be going mad.

I read Lady Durand's letter over and over again. I keep it here in the pages of this book, where from time to time I examine it to see if there is a clue, any kind of clue, about the man who will visit me here. Is he an old farmer? Or an elderly squire? There must be a terrible reason why he was willing to talk to Lady Durand about me. But I cannot imagine what it might be.

Sometimes I find my mind wandering in a very unhelpful direction. I have promised myself that I will have no secrets from you, dear Booke, so here is the truth: Sometimes...sometimes...sometimes I wonder if I should just accept the marriage Lady Durand has arranged for me. Perhaps it is an easier fate than trying to make it on my own.

And then something inside of me breaks and screams NO!

I am so afraid of the promises of men. Isn't that where my mama went wrong? What did Papa say to her to get her to do what we all know must not be done?

Even Catherine has been betrayed by men. She is not a boy, and her papa has cast her aside because of it. Society has cast her aside and deemed her irrelevant because of it.

I know that I have no power, no money, no one who would help me. It is absurd to imagine that I could survive on embroidered slippers. But are there not those who are even worse off than I? Are there not those without the ability to read and write, who are not of sound mind, who are frail or ill? And yet they survive.

People are stronger than they seem, dear Booke. When I can quiet the voices of doubt in the corners of my mind, I *feel* strong. I feel that I am someone who can survive.

I believe in myself.

But I have never done anything out in the world on my own, save attempting to sell embroidered slippers. I am afraid. But as to what frightens me more, poverty and starvation or the promises of a man, I continue to think that men are worse.

Chapter Thirteen

Yesterday Mr. Clark came to call. Mr. Clark is the man of business who oversees this house in the village of Avoncliff.

I thought it was a polite call, that he just wanted to check up on the house. This is one of the many homes the Durand family owns, and they are mostly scattered all over the north, so these southern properties are an annoyance for Mr. Humphrey, Papa's man of business at Rosemont. Mr. Clark is Papa's London solicitor and handles everything in London and Bath. All the houses are not open and occupied at the same time, so managing the details of the staff and such must be quite a burden. Rosemont is Papa's ducal seat (what a thoroughly obnoxious term that is) and the historic home of all the dukes of Leicester.

But no, Mr. Clark was here to see me at Lady Durand's command. He was very civil, but I did not like what he had to say. Not one bit.

It is as I thought. I am to be part of a financial arrangement. I do not understand the particulars; perhaps Mr. Clark did not think a weak-minded female *could* understand the particulars and did not bother to present them clearly. He rushed through the explanation of the agreement and the kind generosity of Lady Durand, but what I understood very plainly is that I am no longer part of the Durand family.

The man who is to become my husband is a landowner somewhere up north. From this, I assume he is a farmer. I was too horrified to really concentrate when Mr. Clark told me where he is from. This is how Lady Durand aims to get rid of me—I will be sent somewhere far away enough that I cannot possibly cause trouble for Papa or the children.

His name is Roman Dryden, and he is thirty-six years old, but at least he is not a widower with eight children, for which I suppose I must be grateful. He has never been married. And perhaps he is not crazy or cruel. Mr. Clark spoke of him respectfully. He is the second cousin of someone Lady Durand met in London. Actually, it sounded as if Lady Durand knew of Mr. Dryden before that and perhaps even arranged to meet Mr. Dryden's cousin in London to discuss this matter.

(I managed to get out of Mr. Clark that Louisa has not received any offers and does not appear to be near receiving any! Ha! Lady Durand thought I would be the cause of Louisa's lack of success, but it seems Louisa has taken care of her own lack of success. She must be furious!)

No, I have not changed my mind. I do not want to be under the thumb of a man. I do not want to marry Mr. Roman Dryden of Somewhere in the North Country. But at the moment I do not have any alternatives, as I do not have any money.

I have not heard from Catherine for some time now, and I'm afraid to reach out to her, as I know I am nothing but a burden and cannot offer her anything more than simple friendship. I feel awkward about the things I told her, even though she has said many shocking things about her own family. I wonder if we can still be friends. Will she want to have a burden such as myself around her when her own life is so complicated?

I do not know what I can do other than to see what I think of this Mr. Roman Dryden.

He apparently has many sheep. And that is all I know.

Chapter Fourteen

LETTER FROM ROMAN DRYDEN

To Miss Lydia Barrow, Stonemeadow House, Avoncliff

Greetings.

My name is Roman Dryden. Perhaps you have heard of me by now through the gracious intervention of Lady Durand. I am writing to ask your leave to call at Stonemeadow House at your convenience to discuss an arrangement, which by now I hope you have considered. I have been in London this past month on business, and Lady Durand gave me leave to courtact you regarding a meeting. I believe I can get to Bath quite easily and thence hire a conveyance to take me directly to Avoncliff. If this arrangement is agreeable to you, I will be in Bath in the first week of November and can be reached at the Bear.

I apologize for the impudence of this communication if you have not yet heard from Lady Durand.

I await word and remain yr servant,

Yrs truly,

Roman Kettering Dryden

Chapter Fifteen

Dearest dearest dearest,

My hands are shaking so dreadfully—

(smeared word)

I must calm down—perhaps I will sneak down to the kitchen for a pot of tea.

Must calm down (blob)

All better now.

(illegible)

I think.

Oh, bother. I have smeared the new start of this letter to you. I will try again. The ink is all over the bottom of my hand, and I drag it across the page as I write.

Let me start again.

I have met him—the one whom Lady Durand has paid to marry me. He wrote me a letter, and I did not know how to answer, but

Lady Durand sent him to stay in Bath, and he wrote to say that he would like to meet me.

My natural instinct was to not reply, to hide, to hope he would just go away. But it disturbed me that there was a man somewhere in Bath awaiting my answer. It felt terrible and invasive, somehow, that some stranger was thinking thoughts in my direction, having been consulted by Lady Durand. I wondered what he had been told about me, what I sounded like when described by someone whose life has been spoiled by my very existence.

For I am too realistic not to understand that my existence must be a source of much anguish for Lady Durand and the family. Who on earth could love a child like myself, the visible result of the worst betrayal possible?

So I did reply, and I told Mr. Dryden that I did not mind meeting him. He came today.

I met him in the library. He had already been shown in, and I was in a panic because I had been indecisive about what to wear, and I wasn't sure if I had made the right decision. I did not want to wear one of Louisa's old gowns, but they are all so much nicer than mine, so I wore the rose pink with all the tiny vines and flowers embroidered on the sleeves. I do not know if rose pink is a good color for me, but I did enjoy working on the embroidery. If only Mme Allard would let me put my designs on her dresses...

I beg your pardon. I'm so nervous, my mind is racing. Back to Mr. Dryden...

He was tall, very tall, standing at the bookcase and looking at the books. I must admit I have never looked at the books. I am not much of a reader. And the books in that room are so old and dusty. I can't imagine who has read them. I don't know who comes here or for what reason. The house isn't in Bath proper. This is a small country town. And while it is a very fine home, it cannot compare to Rosemont. I cannot imagine any of the Durands living here. Perhaps they conquered another family hundreds of years ago and took all of their land...

I'm sorry! I promise I will not get distracted again!

Where was I? Oh, yes. Tall. He is very tall! I am tall for a girl, but he is much taller. I had to crane my neck to speak to him. He has wild, curly hair, which had been tied back but was beginning to tumble free of its riband. I must have been staring, because he put his hand up to touch his hair and begged my pardon for his unruly appearance. I was never so mortified in my life!

He is not handsome, not exactly. He is much older than I and has tanned skin, as if he is often outdoors. Even his clothes had the look of being blown about by the wind. His eyes are grayish green, and he has a strong nose. He does not seem to care for fashion and wore riding clothes that were good quality but plain. Everything was brown, in fact. I nearly asked him why he did not wear any color but brown, but that would have been an impertinence.

Even though I earn money by doing fine needlework, I did not find his simple clothing offensive. Though I confess my heart sings when I am choosing embroidery silks and thinking about how I can change the fall of a skirt to better show off the lace edge, I would rather someone dress plainly than in something expensive but ugly. I almost made this comment in front of Mme Allard once, in fact, and stopped myself just in time! She was at that moment showing me a horrible brown spencer jacket trimmed with gold braid and crowing that she would charge a great deal for it. It looked almost like something a naval officer might wear, it was so heavy and ornate. Dreadful! The fact is, better plain than overdecorated, which is Mme Allard's main problem, unfortunately.

But getting back to Mr. Dryden, he looked strong and honest. I will admit that there was something sweet about his way of hesitating before starting a sentence. His gaze was frank, and he did not attempt to woo me with pretty phrases. He seemed shy, in fact; perhaps he has not spent much time with ladies. Master Howard and his useless Oxford friends often brag about their conversations with various females, and it always sounds as if they are full of witty banter. This was very far from witty repartee!

I'm sorry, I've distracted myself again. I'm mortified to report that as I stood before Mr. Dryden, I did not know what to say, Booke! I did not know what to say. I am not often tongue-tied; Lady Durand would agree. Just think of the many times I have been chided for my wickedly pert comments and slapped because of my ungovernable tongue! And yet today I could barely utter a word.

I am taking deep breaths...my hands are still trembling.

He wishes to marry me, dear Booke. He spoke quite bluntly and begged my pardon for the obvious discomfort it caused me. He did not mention money, although I know from Mr. Clark that Lady Durand has arranged with Papa to pay him. He merely said that Lady Durand is a friend of someone in his family and that he has lately been thinking he would like to get married.

How awkward it was! Every time I looked at him, I wanted to apologize for subjecting him to my scrutiny. And I'm sure he felt the same. He paid me one or two very pleasant compliments, and it seemed he did admire me. I cannot say for sure, of course—he did not seem to be practiced at flattering ladies—but I believe I looked well enough and that he was satisfied I was not some ancient snaggletoothed governess Lady Durand was trying to fob off on him.

It was very strange—he wanted to know what I like to do. I had no answer to this. Like to *do*? When I did not reply, he offered by way of example that he was fond of reading and collecting books. He pointed to the bookcase and opined that I must be a great reader to have such books in my library. Well! You must know how I stammered. I was quite flustered. Does he not know my connection to the duke? Surely he must! I do not own anything in this house, other than the money in my purse from the slippers; I do not even own anything I wear. My entire life, everything has come from the duke.

Then, of course, he became flustered because I was flustered. Two sadly socially maladroit people we were! If I had been watching from afar, I suppose I might have laughed. Two sad sacks, trying to be normal.

He left soon after. I suppose he will write to Lady Durand and tell her whether he still wishes to marry me.

You are wondering whether *I* wish to marry *him*?

I confess, a life as a respectable wife seems very attractive when I contemplate a life of scraping together money from the sales of slippers. But I am afraid, dear Booke. I am afraid of being under someone's control, afraid of having to keep any man happy enough not to harm me.

I really do not know what to do. I wish Catherine were here with me. If I had the courage to reach out to her, I would. But I do not wish to cause her trouble.

Chapter Sixteen

MY DEAREST BOOKE,

I have been very bad. I beg your pardon most sincerely for neglecting you. I have so much to tell you.

I have seen Mr. Dryden twice since he first came to call. He has now returned to London, where he is transacting some sort of business on behalf of his farm. Yes, he is a farmer in the area around Nottingham. My geography is dreadful, so I am not sure where exactly this is, but I believe it is not altogether very far from Rosemont. This makes sense, as he says he has some sort of family connection to the Durands.

However, he is not like any farmer I have ever met. He is educated. A gentleman. You would never know from his speech that he is from so far north, either. He said his family originally hails from Yorkshire. I saw how he spoke so pleasantly to Mrs. Clabbard, who is head over ears in love with him, I dare say.

On his second visit, we went walking around the village; we ended up going much farther from the house than we intended, and I didn't realize how much time had passed until I was shivering with cold. He gave me his jacket because my teeth were chattering. I was so humiliated! That will teach me to take a walk without sufficient wraps!

He explained that he owns much land up north and that he both farms and raises a good many sheep. He does not do it all himself, however. He has many who work for him, and he is certainly not in the fields every day, although I can tell from his tousled hair and windburned skin that he does not hesitate to spend time outside. He has no concern for his attire, which I must own I approve of. He is so much more the man than Master Howard, who once spent three hours in front of a mirror trying to get his cravat into some particular shape.

But yes, I like him. I like him more than I expected.

On his last visit, he offered me a ring. He took it out of a box that he produced from his coat pocket, and I was so startled I fell back in alarm. He cried out and asked if I was all right...I suppose I must have appeared ready to swoon.

It was a beautiful ring, a posey in the shape of a flower with sparkling gems. At first I stood dumbly and would not take it, but I gazed at it, perhaps in horror, perhaps with a thread of excitement. Then I looked up at poor Mr. Dryden. His face...I cannot explain, but he looked...shattered. His face, which had opened itself to me over these three visits, which I had grown to see as kind and gentle and even handsome, now appeared closed, devastated.

I felt like the most wicked person on earth.

I grabbed his hand and tried to explain...but there was nothing to explain. I am afraid to marry him. I am afraid of Lady Durand's machinations. I had sworn that I would never allow myself to be under the control of any man. But these are not reasons I could say aloud. So I stuttered and gasped like a fish, my hand around his, his hand around that beautiful ring.

He spoke gently, saying that he understood my situation, that Lady Durand had hidden nothing from him, and that he had only honorable intentions. He also understood that this was all very rushed and that I might like some time to reflect. He had meetings with his banker in London and had to return thence on the morrow, but he asked if I would keep the ring as a sign of his promise to do well by me. Not an engagement, he said with emphasis. Just a gift to show that he meant well.

I kept the ring. I did not know how to say no. Booke, it was very wrong of me. I know it was. But when the ring was on my finger—yes, he put it there—I felt it belonged there!

I want to be rid of this plight of not knowing where I belong. If I marry him, I will be Mrs. Lesley Lydia Dryden, wife of Mr. Roman Kettering Dryden of Harcourt Estates in Nottingham. I will have money and a position, and yes, I will be a farmer's wife, so I will doubtless have to work extremely hard at farm tasks, which I confess scares me—but I will want for nothing. And he is kind. I can learn to love him.

He is gone now. This is not an engagement, but oh, dear Booke, I think I want it to be! Is that terrible? Am I making a great mistake?

Oh, how I wish you would speak to me!

Chapter Seventeen

Dearest Booke,

I am miserable. Catherine, my beloved Catherine—she is furious with me.

I have never seen her angry before, although the casual way in which she told me about her papa and all the cruel ways he has punished her for being born female did lead me to believe that a deep, explosive anger lay buried inside her. Only I never supposed that she would unleash this anger onto my head.

I have always been somewhat in her thrall, unable to add much to our conversations except to be amazed by her energy and wit. To be honest, I have often thought that she must very bored indeed to want to spend time with me, but it is true that she has no other female companionship but her haughty dresser, the woman who replaced her governess when she decided she was done with the schoolroom. I do not think I am very interesting, having no knowledge of the world outside Rosemont, no fondness for books, and no hobbies outside of my desperate attempts to sell my needlework.

So I was shocked beyond anything when an excited Catherine was shown into the drawing room where I sat, trying to organize an order of slippers but mostly staring at the new ring on my finger and wondering when I would hear from Mr. Dryden again. She charged across the room with such speed, it was as if her weak leg had absolutely no effect. She shouted over her shoulder to the bewildered maid that we should be left alone.

"Lydia!" she cried. "I am sorry! I have not abandoned you, I promise!" She threw her arms around me with such force I nearly fell over. I could feel her heart racing through her fur-trimmed pelisse, and her normally impeccable coiffure was fuzzy and windswept.

"Oh, dear!" I exclaimed. "Did you ride? It is bitterly cold today! Please sit down! What is wrong?"

"I had to think very carefully about what to do," she said, drawing my arm through hers and sitting down beside me on the sofa. "I was not sure I could take care of all the details myself, and I did not have anyone to ask. But I have done it! We will be free, dear Lydia!"

I had no idea what she was talking about, and it must have showed on my face, for the smile faded from her lips, and she drew back to scrutinize my countenance.

"You did not think I forgot you?" she asked. "I promise you I did not. I thought about you day and night. And as you know, I do not control my own life. There were arrangements I had to make, and I was not sure I could manage them myself. But my papa's man of business has always been fond of me, and he was agreeable to most of what I asked for. Lydia, we are going to London. You must pack right away and keep it a secret. Do not tell that dreadful old housekeeper our plans. You may leave her a letter—I will help you write it—but do not say a word to anyone, or all will be lost. They will come after me, and then we will be in a muddle. After we are settled in London, it will be too late for anyone to stop us, and then we may rest easy."

"London?" I said blankly. "London? Why are we going to London?"

"I am saving you from a terrible future," Catherine said, rather dramatically. I was not sure if she was joking or serious, so I said nothing in response but waited for her to continue. This was apparently not the reaction she had hoped for, so she frowned at me.

"How does this save me from a—" I began, but Catherine pushed me away impatiently and stood up. She began to pace back and forth, going from window to mantelpiece and back to me, her uneven gait gradually fading from my notice. Really, when one got used to it, her infirmity did not deserve much attention at all, I found myself thinking.

"I am disappointed with you," she complained. "I have not slept well in several weeks because I was trying to think of a plan. Ever since I saw the letter your cruel stepmama sent, I have been fretting over the best way to take you away from this place. And once I came up with a plan, I had to put it into place. That was difficult, let me tell you. But I have finally set it up, and you need only pack your things and—"

"But Catherine," I protested, "why London? And why do I have to leave in secret? What is this plan you speak of?"

"As you may imagine, it is impossible for me to make any significant change to my life without causing a great deal of fuss," Catherine said. "That man—you know, my papa—has sent me to stay here because the house belonged to Mama and he wants nothing to do with me. Once in a great while, I return home to Albrook, but I do not see him. He does not want to see me, nor does he want me to be seen in society, as I am crippled. But I realized that if you are with me, I can go to London, and London is so big that we can disappear. We need not consort with the people who agree with Papa and will make our lives miserable. I will be able to make the great change in my life that I have been hoping for."

"Disappear?" I gasped.

"Yes," Catherine said. "I have plenty of money and more than a few friends in London. After you showed me your stepmama's letter, I wrote to a friend. He will make introductions for us, and it will all be very proper because you will be my chaperone, and I will be your employer."

Chaperone! Employer! I felt my mind reeling. What was she talking about?

"I have long been wanting to escape!" she was saying. "And now I can do you a good turn also. Your family will not care what happens to you, I imagine. You can write to the duke, your papa, and assure him that you are well—but only if you wish."

"But—but Catherine—" I stammered, "I don't understand what this means."

Catherine laughed. "What this means, dear one, is that you will be free of the Durands forever. You will be in my employ, and you will be independent of any man who wishes to control you. You and I will lead the lives we wish to lead! We will stay in London until everyone has understood that this is what you wish. If we were to try to execute this scheme here at Wansdyke, I'm afraid Lady Durand would most certainly interfere. She does not want you in London, as she thinks you will create a problem for...what is her name?"

"Louisa," I supplied.

"Yes, Louisa. But we will be far away from Lady Durand and her precious Louisa. My friend does not socialize in those circles, so there is no fear that we will run into Lady Durand or Louisa in London. We will wait until her anxiety about you has been assuaged—perhaps all we need do is to wait until Louisa has finally made a match—and then we can return to Wansdyke and do whatever we please, forever! Do you like Bath, Lydia?"

I did not know how to reply. It was not the way I had expected to live my life, as a servant. However, it was an answer to the question I constantly asked myself: Who am I, and where do I belong? Catherine herself had pointed out that she took precedence over me. And Lady Durand had found a farmer for me to marry. I did not belong in a gentlewoman's world, it seemed.

If I could trust Catherine, I would be forever free of this terrible in-between space in which I was raised.

On the other hand, I could marry Mr. Dryden.

Did I trust him? Whom did I trust more: Mr. Dryden, who was being paid by Lady Durand to marry me? Or Catherine, who wanted to help me, but who was also counting on me to free her from the yoke of her father's hatred?

Catherine saw my indecision and thought I was upset about being relegated to a servant's role. She hastened to tell me that she would treat me as a companion, not as a servant, and that she would pay me wages far above what her household servants earned. She did not want me to worry that she felt herself above me in any way—precedence was stupid, she said scornfully. It was merely convenient that she could claim higher rank, because otherwise her scheme would not work. It was fortunate indeed that my background made it possible for her to invite me into her household, she said happily.

"I have not had a governess for some time," she said. "It has been awkward for me not to have a gentlewoman living with me as a companion, but I have not liked any of the options. They were all old, cross-eyed nags."

This made me laugh, but I was still worried. It was then that I made the mistake of telling her the truth. I never, never should have done that. I didn't realize, I suppose, the depth of Catherine's need, that she saw more of a way out for herself in this proposed arrangement than for me.

"I have met Mr. Dryden," I told her, "and he seems very pleasant. I do not know what I should do…"

At first, Catherine simply stood, looking confused. Then understanding spread over her face, followed by fury. She took a step toward me, and I drew back, even though I was seated on a sofa and could not have retreated.

"He is a MAN, Lydia. A man! If you marry him, he will own you. You will have no way out. Look at what that man has done to me. Look at what he can do. And look at what use I am, what little use we are, in this terrible world!"

"He seems very pleasant," I repeated helplessly. I was twisting his ring around and around on my finger, and Catherine's sharp eye caught sight of it. She came to me and grabbed my hand.

"Has he bought you with cheap lies and trinkets?" she cried. "This is what they do, Lydia! You mustn't fall victim! You mustn't believe what he says!"

I was so confused, both by my own heart and by her anger. She frightened me. Her blue eyes blazed with the strength of her emotion, and the edges of the ring cut into my finger. I have answered back to Lady Durand many times and been slapped for it, but I was speechless in the face of Catherine's fury. I had never seen her like this, and I did not know how to respond.

Catherine is my only friend. She is the only person who has ever genuinely cared for me, except perhaps for Marianne, who is not very bright and of course remains devoted to her mama. I am so afraid to lose her. And she is right, of course. If I marry Mr. Dryden, I will be in his power forever.

But do I want to be a servant? And this terrible anger of Catherine's—I had never seen it before. What if we disagree on things? I have never been a compliant girl. Will we quarrel dreadfully?

I just do not know.

Catherine left soon after, saying coldly that she had thought better of me. It occurred to me that perhaps she was more upset about her own freedom being spoiled than about my possible subjugation by Mr. Dryden. Then I shook free of the thought, which was quite unfair of me. Both of us are unfortunate women, after all. One person's misery is not better or worse than another's.

I just do not know what to do.

Your devastated friend,

Lydia

Chapter Eighteen

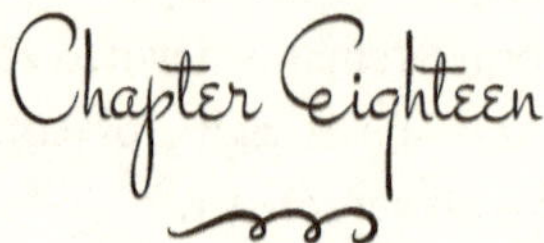

Letter from Roman Dryden

c/o Mr. Dwight, Fenchurch Street, London

To Miss Lydia Barrow, Stonemeadow House, Avoncliff

My dear Miss Barrow,

I hope you are well. My journey was without complication, and I have returned to the home of my man of business here on Fenchurch Street. It is a busy neighborhood where activity starts early and ends late, but it is convenient to the warehouses and commercial suppliers I must visit.

I hope you do not feel pressured or inconvenienced by this letter. I do not mean to ask for your reply any earlier than you wish to give it. Please forgive me if I say that you have a fair countenance that no man would easily be able to forget. I keep thinking of how much you would like Harcourt House, how much it could use a female presence, and how eager I am to show it to you.

But then, this sounds like I am trying to talk you into something that you may not want at all! Forgive me. I merely wish to tell you that I am well and that I hope you are happy. You may reach me anytime at Fenchurch Street while I await the completion of my business here in London and thereafter at Harcourt House just outside of Newark-on-Trent.

Yr servant obd'ly,

Roman Dryden

Chapter Nineteen

My dearest Booke,

You are always here for me, and I do not know what I would do without you.

Mr. Dryden has written to me with his London address. I have not written back, as I do not know what to say. I feel terrible.

I have taken off his ring, as I feel I have no right to wear it. We are not engaged, and he says in his letter that he does not wish to pressure me into an answer. He is a very busy man, and I believe him when he says that his farm operations keep him well occupied. I am certainly not the only thing on his mind.

I admit I am torn between accepting his proposal and throwing in my lot with Catherine, whom I trust has my best interests at heart. At least, I *believe* she has my best interests at heart.

Otherwise why would she befriend someone like myself? Why would a person who is so beautiful and filled with such vivacity want to be my friend except because she likes me? And why would she want to serve me an ill turn? Whereas I can think of many reasons why a man might want to arrange with Lady Durand to marry me, such as gaining a free housekeeper and bedmate. I do not think most men are looking for friendship from their wives.

Catherine understands where I come from. What can Mr. Dryden possibly know about the precarious situation in which I have always lived? Who knows what bits and pieces of the truth Lady Durand has shared with him in order to get him to marry me?

He may think he knows my story, but surely she has shaped it in whatever way is convenient for her purpose. All Lady Durand wants is for someone to cart me far, far away from London and Rosemont so that I will never be in the public eye or disgrace Papa's name or those of her children.

I suppose both Catherine and Mr. Dryden are self-interested. It is not completely out of charity that either is willing to help me.

Is that bad, however? I do not want charity, I have to admit. In either case, as a wife or as Catherine's companion, I will work. These are both honorable options.

Whom do I trust, however? That is the question, and while I can explore the recesses of my mind in your pages, I know that there is no firm answer.

One thought entered my mind the other day as I sat drawing another design for a dress the Bath dressmaker will probably never allow me to work on.

My mama trusted Papa, and she should not have.

Have I told you about my mama, dearest Booke? It is too sad a story to dwell on, but I am determined not to keep anything from you. She is still alive, you know. I have not seen her in many years and have determined that I shall never see her, ever. It is better that way, as I do not think she would be happy to see me, and digging into those past hurts will only cause me pain.

She does not live with my legal papa, Mr. Jonathan Barrow, but at a convalescent home that my real papa arranged for her. It is something of a secret, as it would not do for people to find out that Papa is keeping her locked away. But she is not well, and I have heard Louisa telling Marianne that she wanders the grounds in her shift. Perhaps that is a false story concocted to shame me. I would not put it past Louisa to create such a tale, although she insisted to Marianne that she overheard this detail one evening when Lady Durand was quarreling with Papa about the money he was spending to keep my mama in that place.

Surely she has forgotten me by now.

When I think of what Papa did to Mama, I think I cannot marry. I cannot trust a man, ever. And Catherine's willingness to take me into her household makes my heart swell with affection. Two ladies supporting each other forever, having been rejected by the men in their lives—surely nothing could be better! I would never have to worry about being abandoned or alone.

But I have not heard from Catherine since she left in such anger. I believe I must make the first move and ask her to forgive me. But will she see me?

I do not know. I fear that if I try to see her, she will reject me. Then there will be no choice but for me to marry Mr. Dryden.

While I love Catherine with all my heart, I will always remain most affectionately yours, your devoted friend,

Lydia

Chapter Twenty

TODAY I WENT to see Catherine. I took some of her favorite cakes from a shop in Bath. It was raining rather hard, and there was such a bitter, chilly wind! I managed to keep the cakes dry, which was quite a feat.

I was also in Bath to see Mme Allard, who had asked me to call. It seems that she is quite rushed to finish several gowns, and she asked if I was available to sew the lace trim on one of them. I am very proud of myself, for she looked down her nose at me and offered me quite a mean sum to do the work, and I looked down my nose at her and refused.

Before you gasp and say I should not have done so, be assured that she is paying me double what she originally offered because I demanded it! Oh, I was as polite as can be. But I offered to do more than she had asked, not just to attach the lace but to embroider little green leaves on the sleeves. I happened to have a linen handkerchief I could show her with the same pattern along with rosebuds. I suggested that we omit the rosebuds, as the color of the gown would not have gone well with them.

Then I told her my price, and she agreed instantly. I could see her counting up her profits in her head, as she would be able to charge quite a bit more for a gown with this kind of decoration. And the lady who wants it is someone of consequence who is in Bath due to ill health. I was so proud of myself.

I believe it was not just my skill that swayed her, however. When I arrived, she was at first disinclined to see me, for she was hunting frantically for a piece of quite beautiful and expensive French lace that had already been measured and cut. She had misplaced it, you see...and you well know that I am superior at finding lost items! Yes, I found the missing piece—it had affixed itself to the back of her gown. She must have sat on it! After that, I believe she would have bought anything at all from me!

You might be asking why I am bothering with the sewing, since I can marry Mr. Dryden if I wish. Well, I have not heard from him since that last letter. It is true that I have not written back, for I know not what to say. He may or may not still be in London.

And Catherine...well, I went to visit her after purchasing the cakes and my successful visit to Mme Allard. And she would not see me. This has never happened before.

I was told that she was not feeling well and was not seeing visitors. It is true that sometimes when it rains, her leg pains her. But the Catherine I know rides her horse at top speed through the mud! So I am doubtful that rain would cause her so much pain that she would not see me.

I think she has decided I am not worth the bother.

I am sadder than you can imagine. She has been my one true friend, even if we have only known each other these few short autumn months.

It seemed that at one time, I had both Mr. Dryden and Catherine, and now I may have neither. It's as if I were served up too many choices, and now God takes them away from me because I don't deserve them. Although I own I think it is rather dramatic of Catherine to be too angry even to see me. And the cakes! I have been eating them myself!

I wish I could share them with you,

Lydia

Chapter Twenty-One

Dear Booke,

I went to see Catherine again, but she would not see me.

I am so lonely.

I am thinking of writing to Mr. Dryden. Is that a mistake, I wonder? I do not know what to say. Do I ask about his business in London? Do I mention Lady Durand? I have no thoughts on this matter.

I am absolutely miserable.

Yours ever,

Lydia

Chapter Twenty-Two

My dear Booke,

It is December. I think I will be spending Christmas alone here in this terrible, empty house. I have heard nothing from Lady Durand. I have heard nothing from Catherine. I think our friendship is over indeed, and I will ever be alone.

My shoes have sold well, and I have also sold many handkerchiefs. Mme Allard grudgingly agrees that my designs are better than hers, and she has begun allowing me a free hand with some of her most expensive dresses. I have accumulated some savings. But none of this gives me any pleasure.

My isolation in this house is driving me mad. I never thought I would miss Master Howard, but I confess that I would even welcome the sight of him, I am so lonely and desperate for a friendly face.

It is strange that I had no inkling of how lonely I would feel in this house when I first arrived. I was often alone at Rosemont, but I suppose I was surrounded by people and chose not to interact with them. I thought that I liked being alone. But to have loneliness imposed on one is another matter entirely.

I believe it is because I met Catherine and know what it is like to have a friend.

And I believe it is because I met Mr. Dryden and know what it is like to be admired.

It is like a disease! Will I never rid myself of these unlucky associations? Why is it that a taste of happiness makes me hate my life?

I will write to Mr. Dryden tonight. I will find something to say. I do not know if he is in London, but he promised to let me know if he was leaving, so he may still be there. Perhaps my letter will reach him.

At least I can rely on your friendship, can I not?

Dearest Booke!

I will remain your loving Lydia forever.

Chapter Twenty-Three

Letter from Marianne Durand

Rosemont

Lydia darling,

I miss you more than you will ever know. But I am writing this letter in haste, so forgive me if I do not tell you what is happening here at Rosemont or ask how you do.

I heard from Louisa today. Her Season does not go well. She says there are heiresses she cannot compete with. Mama is telling her to encourage the advances of some odious man with FOUR children. He is a marquess who wears spectacles and reads books. Louisa is very upset. But this is not what I wanted to tell you.

Louisa says that Mama has arranged a marriage for you with a farmer from some distant village up north. Oh, Lydia, you mustn't! Please do not! Louisa said many things that scared me, and I fear this man may be neither decent nor honest.

I have heard that he is hungry for land and is lurking about London, looking for a rich wife who will allow him to acquire more property. He apparently wishes this new wife to serve as his housekeeper so that he need not spend money on wages, so she will be forced to cook and clean. Lydia also says she suspects he is already in a relationship with some disreputable lady in London—Mama let slip that he spends much time in London, even though his primary activity is supposedly farming.

I am afraid this man is duplicitous and miserly and that there is something odd about the way he is looking for a wife. Why would a farmer from the north be in London looking for a wife unless he had something—or perhaps many things—to hide?

Do not be angry with me, but I showed Louisa's letter to Howard, who is home from Cambridge, and even he was appalled. He took it upon himself to demand the story from Papa—I certainly would not have had that courage, but as he is Papa's heir, perhaps he felt Papa would not be angry with him. But he got nothing useful from Papa, who said that Mama was merely looking out for your interest.

Louisa said this is all about erasing you from the family so that you cannot interfere with our happiness. Dearest Lydia, this is the most absurd thing I have ever heard, and my heart aches that Louisa says such wicked things.

I wrote to her right away and scolded her; if I am honest, she did not sound displeased at the thought of you disappearing, which I believe is due to the stress of not having a successful London Season. I simply do not believe Louisa is as horrible as her words make her sound. But if even one of these shocking things is true, then you are in danger!

What can I do to persuade you not to marry him?

Louisa says that Mama has paid him a great sum and has also given him some lands near his own. She says that he is old, tanned, and works outside all day.

I am scared, Lydia! Louisa thought it was all very funny, but Howard and I think it is a very bad thing indeed!

Will you be home at Christmas? We miss you so terribly. Howard tries to deny it, but he misses you, too.

Please write back!

Yours ever so faithfully and with much affection,

Marianne

Chapter Twenty-Four

Dear Booke,

Several shocking things have happened.

I had a letter from Marianne, which I will keep in these pages. 'Tis unfortunate that I wrote to Mr. Dryden before her letter arrived. It was not a long letter that I sent, but I told him I hoped to see him one day soon and that I was grateful for his attentions. In other words, I was not declining his advances, certainly.

But after reading Marianne's letter, I think I must have been tricked...although he is not the wrinkled, tanned old man that she claims. It is strange, but I did not see him at all in the way she described.

Certainly he dresses plainly enough that perhaps it could be considered a sign of frugality, which is a better way of describing someone than using a word like "miser." It is true that his wife will have to depend on the money he chooses to give her, and having a miserly husband would be a very trying experience. But he did not ask me any questions about my housekeeping abilities. Indeed, I was embarrassed that he thought I was better read than I am.

Perhaps Lady Durand has already told him I am able to do most of what the housekeeper does? I am certainly no fool, though I am not competent in a kitchen at all, and I am astonished that anyone would think I could do the jobs of a cook and housekeeper at the same time. That is a risk indeed, not only for me but for any idiot of a man who thinks he can easily find a woman to do both jobs competently at once and who won't either starve him or poison him.

I do admit that there is something odd about him being in London to look for a wife. That part is disturbing, but I do not have enough experience with London to know why anyone would do such a thing. But isn't it extreme to suppose that he could only be in London to maintain a liaison with a lady?

Perhaps not. I must be naïve.

In any case, I always knew Lady Durand had paid him to marry me. In that sense, I am not naïve.

I was just so lonely, I think I saw what I wanted to see. I had hoped that whatever his motivation, it would save me from a life of worry over selling enough slippers to ladies in more fortunate circumstances.

I've decided that I will not marry Mr. Dryden. That was a fantasy, and it was wrong of me to fall for it.

I have been wavering, going back and forth between my hope that his regard is sincere and my belief that Catherine's fit of temper was because she could see objectively what I could not, that I was falling prey to a man's attentions and would suffer as a result. Her outburst worried me, but it makes sense that her panic and distress over Mr. Dryden was because she feared the very foundation of our friendship—our bond over being abandoned daughters—was being destroyed.

Marianne's letter helped me to come to my senses. The arrangement with Mr. Dryden is filled with questions that even Master Howard cannot answer, and he is the one with the most power to get information from my papa. If even Master Howard thinks something is amiss, then the answer is clear. I must ask Catherine to forgive my momentary delusion and forge ahead with her plan.

After reading Marianne's letter, I went to see Catherine and had another shock. I had not seen her since that day a fortnight ago, when she was so very angry at me. I have tried to visit on several occasions, but she would not see me, claiming to be too ill for guests, which I do not believe for a minute. Today, however, I wanted to tell her that I would not marry Mr. Dryden after all, that she had been right all along about not trusting my life to a man.

Here is the shock. When I arrived, I found her with...a man. She introduced him as her cousin, but he burst out laughing when she said this, and Catherine looked quite mischievous. No one else was there, and he put his arm around her when he thought I wasn't looking. He had a French accent and was very handsome, although in that girlish way that I generally do not care for. I could almost swear he rouged his cheeks, but the light was not good, as the weather was abominable.

I am not sure how she was able to sit with him without a chaperone, although it is possible it was the tiresome old dresser's day off. She begged my pardon quite prettily for not being able to see me when I visited last, and when I tried to explain about Mr. Dryden, she interrupted me with a wave of her hand and went back to her silly conversation with this French cousin of hers. They were exchanging jokes, but much of it was in French, so I did not understand it. I believe that the jokes were quite dirty. They sounded like the kind of humor the kitchen boy at Rosemont liked. But I would not know.

I was quite put out, as I had hoped to deliver my news about Mr. Dryden and repair the rift between Catherine and myself, and instead I was forced to listen to giggling and dirty French jokes for an hour. I finally got up to leave, and Catherine insisted on walking me to the door. Thank goodness, she left her French friend behind, and I was able to tell her hastily that I would not marry Mr. Dryden.

She had hushed me earlier, but as we stood at the door, her eyes softened and filled with tears.

"You did this for me, dear Lydia?"

In truth, I hadn't...I'd done it for *me*, because Marianne was looking after me from afar. But my heart was full because the expression on her face was so kind. I threw my arms around her and did not disagree with her statement.

"Now, now," she said, holding me tight. "You are my one true friend, Lydia Barrow! I will never let you go. And you shall never have cause to regret your choice. Trust me. I will come to see you tomorrow, and all will be well."

I am feeling a jumble of things right now! I am sad about Mr. Dryden but relieved that I did not fall into a bad scheme. I am happy that Catherine is still my friend, but I did not like that Frenchman touching her. I am sad that I am clearly not invited to spend Christmas at Rosemont, but I am glad that I do not have to deal with Louisa or Lady Durand.

I must put my head down like the ox in the field and work, work, work. I will create beautiful designs and show Mme Allard that I deserve to be paid well for what I can do. Only when I have money can I have independence.

And of course, I will always be affectionately YOURS, dear Booke.

Chapter Twenty-Five

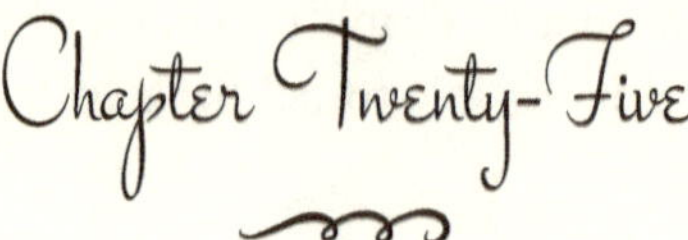

Dearest, dearest Booke,

Just a few words before I pack you away, for we are off to London at dawn. I will write more when we are there.

Catherine is taking me to London. The day after that very strange visit to her house (I saw the Frenchman peeking out at me after I'd left and was standing outside waiting for the cart to be brought round—so odd! And then Catherine appeared to yank him away, and they disappeared behind the draperies), she called on me, and this is what transpired.

She said that I should leave this house before Lady Durand forces me to marry Mr. Dryden and that she would help me avoid this fate. I became flustered. I have not yet written to Mr. Dryden that I will not marry him, and to be frank, I am afraid to write this letter. Every time I sit down and tell myself I owe him a reply, I conjure up his kindly face and cannot lift the pen. I recall what Marianne wrote to me and try again to pick up the pen, but still I cannot.

When I think of what Lady Durand will say when I tell her I refuse to marry Mr. Dryden, my stomach turns into a knot and the blood runs cold in my veins. She has the power to turn me out of this and any other property Papa owns.

I have nothing but my needlework skills to save me, and at the moment it is not enough to live on. All my connections are in Bath, and if Lady Durand seeks to ruin me, I could not stay in Bath. I would have to start over elsewhere, and the thought of approaching shops where I am not known in a town where I am not known again is just horrible.

Yes, I have considered that perhaps I could apply for lodging somewhere in Bath, but I don't even know where to start. At times like this, I find that the supposed "kindness" of being taken in and raised by Lady Durand was actually not a kindness at all but a sort of cruelty.

In many ways, I received similar benefits to the rest of the Durand children, even though Lady Durand never liked me and said mean things to me. But being raised in the country at the ducal seat meant that I never learned what I needed to know in order to become savvy and support myself. I am about as helpless as Louisa and Marianne, except perhaps that I always knew in the back of my mind that Lady Durand would always take care of them but not me.

It took me a while to realize that other than marriage, there was no way for me to leave that household without starving. And it took me even longer to come up with this feeble scheme of selling my needlework. I had hoped to eventually save enough money and make enough connections in town to find my way, but it is too soon.

I know Catherine wants to help me. I know she believes that we women must be strong and stand up for each other, but in fact most women owe their situations to the men in their lives, which means they cannot be trusted to help each other. They have no independence.

Even Catherine has no independence, though at least her father can scarcely turn her out of the house. I, on the other hand, legally have nothing to do with the Durands. My name is Barrow despite the fact that Jonathan Barrow is not my father. Lady Durand could easily turn me out of the house, and I suppose she is doing me a kindness by giving me to Mr. Dryden.

Catherine is doing the best she can to help me, that much is clear. She will protect me as much as she is able, and she has considerably more money and influence than I. She has told me that while I will not want for anything, I may choose to continue sewing and designing fine patterns for sale so that I will have something of my own and not feel that my life is dedicated to serving. She is earnest about this, the idea that I should have something of my own.

I suppose this is what I have always intended by writing my thoughts down for you, dear Booke. It is important for a woman to have a place that is her own, and for me it has been the pages of my pocket books. I plan to accumulate enough savings that if some disaster were to strike, I might still be able to go out on my own.

So I am rushing to pack, as Catherine thinks we should leave at first light tomorrow. I am to go with her as her companion, so she is not taking any of the maids at Wansdyke. She says that after things have quieted down, we can return to Wansdyke, and I will never, never again have to deal with Lady Durand or any of the rest of my family.

I don't know exactly how I feel about this. Marianne will be relieved that I am not marrying Mr. Dryden, but she will be heartbroken to never see me again. However, there is no other way, as I have come to understand. If I defy Lady Durand, I must remove myself forever from that world.

I have mixed feelings about never returning to Rosemont, never seeing Marianne again. I even feel strange about never seeing Louisa or Master Howard again. And Papa? I don't know. When I see his face, I am reminded that the hard lines of his nose and chin are my own. But it also hardly seems to matter, as he doesn't spare me much thought. I feel more distress at the thought of never again seeing my bedroom at Rosemont.

Sensibility makes no sense! The things that tug at my heart are not the things society says are important.

Oh, dear Booke, I am afraid. But I cannot see what else to do. I trust Catherine. I believe she is as strong and as bold as she seems. Her father takes no interest in her, so I do not worry that he will thwart this plan. But I expect never to live at Stonemeadow House again.

No matter what happens, I will ever, ever, be yours affectionately,

Lydia

Chapter Twenty-Six

HAPPY CHRISTMAS, dear, dear Booke!

Everything has been a whirlwind, and I beg your pardon very much for neglecting you!

We are at Claverton House, which is the official residence of Catherine's papa when he is in London. She says he never comes here, that he says London makes him ill, but the truth is that he hates feeling as if people pity him because the earldom will disappear upon his death.

She is so matter-of-fact about this, I find it astonishing. She also says she thinks he should take another wife, but I can see from the set of her chin that she is lying. She does not want him to remarry in order to sire an heir. I have to admit, the thought does cause me to shiver, even though it is a common enough thing. But it makes me feel as if a child is but a piece of merchandise to be bartered and sold...

Then again, what am I, pray tell?

Some mornings, I wake up and feel a few moments of painful anxiety because I'm not sure where I am and thoughts of Bath shopkeepers are drifting through my mind. It takes a while for me to realize that I am staring at the ceiling of my room in Claverton House, that there is a distant clattering outside the window on the streets of London, that I am safe, and that I have a friend who will not abandon me.

I had not realized how worried I was every single second of every single day. It was taking a toll on me, and I didn't even realize that this steady hum of worry was changing the temperature of my existence. But here in London, no one is plotting to get rid of me or oppress me. Life feels almost mundane, and I love that it has become so.

I have fallen quite easily into the role of Catherine's companion. It seems like a dream, but we are settling into a comfortable pattern, one that can be sustained forever. I suppose I need not have worried. Catherine planned everything perfectly.

There is only minimal staff here, as the house is always empty, but the housekeeper has been kind enough toward me, treating me more like Catherine's friend than her paid companion. Yes, paid! Catherine insists on paying me. I am embarrassed to discuss money, but she pays me more than I could ever earn doing needlework.

On the other hand, I have had to purchase many new items, as I cannot be seen in Louisa's old dresses, which Catherine very kindly told me are quite out of date. I would not have known such a thing, of course, but she took me to her modiste and ordered a number of garments for me. I was horrified at the cost, but Catherine waved away my concern and said I could repay her in the future.

I know nothing of London society, but it does not matter, as Catherine does not attend most of the functions someone such as Louisa would be desperate to gain entrance to. I thought it was because of her weak leg, but then I realized it was stupid of me to think so.

Catherine does not care who sees her limp. She is always the one who decides whether a person is a waste of time or a worthy acquaintance. For this, I respect her. She is right, of course.

However, I am concerned by the visitors who have come to see her. They seem...odd. I do not know how to explain the uneasy feeling they give me. They dress strangely, and some are émigrés who don't speak English. They are all very polite, but sometimes Catherine does not call me in when they are here, and I wonder that she agrees to see them without a chaperone. While I am not very worldly, I know that Lady Durand would not allow Marianne to sit alone with any of these visitors.

There is to be a dinner party tonight with some of her friends, and the cook came to me to ask if I would approve the menu. I, approve a menu? Most of the dishes had French names, so I could not offer my opinion.

Catherine gave me a pair of diamond earrings for Christmas. She said they were an old pair she has lost interest in, but sometimes I think she invents excuses to prevent me from refusing a gift. I purchased a very pretty pair of gloves and embroidered one of my rosebud patterns on them for her, but obviously they could not measure up to diamond earrings! I was embarrassed, but she exclaimed so loudly over the gloves that I was quite touched.

One more thing, dear Booke...I am going to write to Roman Dryden. It is not fair that I have made my decision and kept it from him. I will write him now, before I lose my courage. And I will return his ring, though I do not know how to send it to him. If he is still in London, I suppose I can meet with him, although I should take someone with me, if I am concerned about propriety... which I suppose I am. But I am more concerned about Catherine losing her temper with me if she hears that I am going to see Mr. Dryden. So I will go in secret, and I will not tell Catherine about my visit until the deed is done.

I have not told Marianne my decision or anything about my trip to London, as Catherine has told me not to say anything to any of the Durands until it is clear that I have declined Mr. Dryden's offer and we have seen Lady Durand's reaction. Once everything has been settled, I will write to Marianne and assure her I am well and that she need not worry about me, despite any rumors she might hear.

Happy, happy Christmas! I feel both relief and sadness at being free of Lady Durand. I have cut myself off from the only home I have ever known, a childhood that was sometimes happy, and the only family I have. Catherine says she is my new family—she doesn't put much stock in blood relations, she says—but I still feel some sadness.

You, however, cannot be replaced. Ever. Ever.

And I am ever yours,

Lydia

Chapter Twenty-Seven

LETTER FROM ROMAN DRYDEN

c/o Mr. Dwight, Fenchurch Street, London

To Miss Lesley Lydia Barrow, Claverton House, Grosvenor Square, London

My dear Miss Barrow,

Please do not apologize. I understand that you may have had a change of heart—or perhaps you were never as decided on the matter as I was, for which I do not blame you.

I am, however, surprised that you are in London. I am caught between joy and disappointment, not knowing in which direction my heart should settle, as I would have been so very happy to see you. Alas, I suppose that is not to be? Or would you find it agreeable to meet with me?

I promise I will not say anything to make you uncomfortable or press my suit. The truth is that I wish to make a clean breast of some matters I fear you may have misunderstood. It is selfish of me to wish for us to part on honest terms, but there it is. If there is anything I dislike, it is when no one tries to right a misunderstanding, for the pain that follows may torment one for years. Do not ask me how I know this. I would like to have an honest conversation with you so that we may each go our own separate way without painful memories of what passed between us.

I will be at this address, if you would be so good as to write to me here. I have been afflicted with a chest ailment—mild, I assure you —and have not been able to return to my properties in the north. I fear I will be here into the new year and perhaps some weeks beyond. I am grateful for your letter and beg you grant me the indulgence of one last meeting.

About the ring, which you very kindly offered to return—I hope you will wear it in good health and consider it a token of affection and respect from one who admires you greatly.

Your most ob't,

Roman Dryden

Chapter Twenty-Eight

My dear Booke,

We have just returned from a Twelfth Night masquerade, and I have so much to say to you.

My head hurts dreadfully, and it is daybreak. I want nothing more than to collapse into bed, but I must unload my woes on you now or I will burst.

Tonight I prevailed upon Catherine to let me act the role of her companion rather than that of her friend and confidant. I am ill at ease at all these dinners and parties, where men keep sidling up to me to say all manner of bizarre and shocking things. I am appalled at the liberties they take. One young man asked me to explain the words to a folk song that was so rude I could barely look him in the eye. Fortunately, the lady on the other side of me scolded him in French and told me not to mind him, as he was quite intoxicated.

Remember how I told you it was almost a cruelty that I was raised by Lady Durand in almost the same way as her daughters? I am finding that I have been very sheltered from the antics of men! I do not know why young ladies enjoy that sort of thing, but I do not! I feel as if I am in the middle of Master Howard's group of infantile friends, but I can't slap anyone. All that slapping practice at Rosemont has done me no good here!

I finally got it through Catherine's head that since she is paying me a wage, I cannot be her friend, or at least not in the way she keeps saying. And I am content to be in her employ. She has saved me from an uncertain future, and I am eternally grateful. I am not proud, and I do not mind if the housekeeper does not know how to speak to me because she cannot tell what my place is. I have lived betwixt and between my whole life, so this is nothing new. What matters to me is that I do not get grabbed by all these young men who wish to flirt. I am not interested and will never be interested. I have made my decision about marriage, and so, I thought, had Catherine.

I do not know what I ate or drank, and I am sure it was very fine, but I was sick to my stomach in the back garden of an enormous residence somewhere in Mayfair. Fortunately, I always have a clean handkerchief in my reticule—I embroider them, so of course I carry them—and I was wiping my face when I saw Catherine and one of the Frenchmen of her acquaintance deep in an embrace in the shadows.

Even worse, it was someone I had introduced to her. He had seemed very kind and very shy, and his English was not good, so I had taken pity on him when I recalled that Catherine's French was very good. He had seemed so gentle and good-hearted, but I suppose men are just men. They are all the same. I very much regret allowing him anywhere near Catherine.

I am so tired and so put out by the whole affair, I am sorry I went. Catherine is being foolish, and I will tell her so as soon as I see her. She was giddy and laughing all the way home in the carriage while I held my head in my hands.

Oh! I will tuck Mr. Dryden's last letter into these pages. I cannot tell you why, but it saddens me. I cannot meet with him—I simply cannot. My resolve would fail me, and Catherine would be so angry. She would tell me that he has some sinister plan to sweep me away and marry me. Remember the letter from Marianne? I cannot trust anyone who plots and connives with Lady Durand.

My head hurts, so I must go lie down.

Chapter Twenty-Nine

Dearest!

I am all out of breath. I still have my hat on, for I dashed into the house and ran straight up the stairs. You will never guess what happened to me today!

I saw Louisa!

It was dreadful. Lady Durand was not with her, but I had the most terrible shock. It was at the milliner's. I was picking up a hat for Catherine that I am going to retrim, since the color really does not suit her complexion but she was determined to have it anyway, as the shape is the same as one she left back at Wansdyke.

Louisa was coming into the shop as I was leaving. She was shocked to see me. I thought I looked particularly well today in one of my new dresses, but Louisa was rude and said I looked pale and wan. I am sure I did not look pale and wan! She was probably annoyed that I looked as well as I did!

I panicked, I must admit. She asked me what I was doing in London, so I told her I was visiting a friend. She began to question me in that aggressive way she has—you know what I mean—and my head was spinning with all the questions, questions, questions. I knew she would report on me to Lady Durand, and I couldn't think of what to say.

Mr. Dryden has surely told Lady Durand that I will not marry him, and I am realizing I was a fool for giving him my direction in London, because Louisa will now tell Lady Durand that I am here, and Lady Durand will ask him where I am staying. I have been so very stupid!

I managed to get away after turning the conversation around to her Season, at which she grew ill-tempered and excused herself to make her purchases. I suppose she is just as luckless as when she first arrived. It serves her right. I am uncomfortable even thinking such a thought, as I know it must be terrible to feel so unwanted. I have felt that way my whole life, and no matter how mean Louisa is to me, I don't wish that on anyone.

I felt a strange combination of anger, relief, and sadness at the thought that by turning down Mr. Dryden and accepting Catherine's kindness, I have excised myself from that family forever. I am still the flesh and blood of Papa, but with this act, I have chosen my future.

Chapter Thirty

Dear Booke, it has finally happened. The disaster I have been afraid of—in fact, too afraid to even admit it here in these pages.

Today Lady Durand came to call. And with just a few very well-chosen words, she informed me that I was an ungrateful wretch for declining Mr. Dryden and that I was not welcome at Rosemont ever again.

One thing I did not anticipate was that I have also been immediately thrown out of the house in Avoncliff. I do not have many belongings, but I left most of my sewing supplies behind, and those are all gone. Everything that I had—gone.

While I knew that I could not continue to reside at Avoncliff, Catherine had assured me that I would live with her at Wansdyke, and I thought I would move the rest of my belongings quickly and quietly once we returned after the holidays. But no. Lady Durand informed me that she has had Mrs. Clabbard (that old witch!) empty my room and dispose of my things. I am sure Mrs. Clabbard was only too delighted to see me cast out of the family in disgrace.

When Lady Durand came, Catherine was not at home, and I was surprised at this coincidence until I realized she must have asked the servants when Catherine would be out. Thus she was able to pretend that she was disappointed not to see Catherine—"dear Lady Catherine," she said, sounding so very syrupy. I'm sure she was very curious, as I am realizing there is much gossip and many rumors circulating concerning Lady Catherine's plight, both because of her limp and because her papa the earl is without an heir. But I think Lady Durand did not want an audience for the many harsh things she said to me.

You must wonder how I faced her! I was strangely calm. Perhaps it was because Catherine has given me the backbone I did not have in the past. Perhaps it was the conviction that I have done the right thing. When I consider how tempted I was to marry Mr. Dryden and how sorry I was to tell him that I would not, my courage begins to fail...except that to maintain my connection with Lady Durand feels impossible. I could not bear to feel that she has made me a hostage by selling me off to Mr. Dryden.

In the end, I think it must have given me courage to know that I was in a place of complete honesty. I was no longer pretending that anything in my life made sense, and when I thought of how Catherine responded to everything in her own life that did not make sense, I realized that I could lift my chin, too.

So I did not cry, and I did not lose my temper. Lady Durand was rude, but she was also clear and to the point. I am not to claim a relationship to papa. I have a name and a legal papa in Barrow. I am not to tell people that I was raised at Rosemont. I am particularly not to tell people that Louisa and Marianne are my sisters, and I am certainly never to claim a relationship with Master Howard. This hurt me, but I kept my composure. (I never liked Master Howard, anyway.)

But at the end of her visit, she said something strange, and I am still pondering her meaning. She was going on about Mr. Dryden and what an ungrateful wretch I was to have refused him. She almost—almost—made it sound as if Mr. Dryden were someone of consequence. Which, of course, is absurd. Though he appeared to be a gentleman, Lady Durand would never have arranged an advantageous marriage for me! What a strange concept, to be sure.

Lady Durand would love to see me reclining in the mud with "my kind," as she put it. And Mr. Dryden himself said he was a farmer, although it did occur to me that it was odd for a farmer to have a man of business in London and for him to spend so much time away from his lands. He had the appearance of a man who spends a good deal of time out of doors and was dressed neatly but not in a stylish manner.

What Lady Durand said was that I was forever causing trouble, that I did not know how to be grateful, and that I was ruining everyone's lives. Isn't that odd? How am I ruining everyone's lives? How is refusing Mr. Dryden related to anyone else's situation?

Bother, I truly wish Catherine had met him. She would have known right away what his story was. Or she would have been bold and simply asked him. When you are the daughter of an earl, it does not occur to you that anything you might say is impertinent.

Hmm, I suppose this is why Louisa is the way she is. But why is it that Louisa annoys me so much and Catherine does not? I suppose it is because Louisa is worried about her consequence, and Catherine is not. How stupid! As if anyone could take Louisa's status away from her!

I am perplexed by Lady Durand's mutterings about Mr. Dryden. But I am glad I did not cry or shout or storm out in a temper. I suppose I have grown more mature since being sent away to Avoncliff? Or perhaps I have Catherine to thank. She likes me for myself and gave me the courage to turn down Mr. Dryden.

Although—and I will admit this ONLY to you, dear heart—thinking of Mr. Dryden still makes me sad. I have not replied to his letter. I feel tied up in knots every time I resolve to sit down and write. I want to return his ring as well. It pains me to look at it, but I am afraid that if I see him, I will betray my feeling.

Yes, I have feelings for him, dear Booke. I cannot help myself. I have never been admired, and even if Mr. Dryden is only being polite, his letter is so very flattering. It makes me crestfallen to realize his is the first and last romantic gesture I will ever receive.

Chapter Thirty-One

D EAREST!

Things keep getting worse. Oh, when will this end? I regret the day I agreed to come to London. No, that's not right. I do not regret it, because I am even more upset to think of Catherine here without me. I am the only protection she has. No one else in the world seems to care whether she lives or dies.

We went to another one of her wild émigré parties, the kind I despise. I did not want to go, as I always come home with the headache, and it turns my days and nights upside down. But I did go, as I am always worried about the rowdiness of the crowds there. There are usually many men and not many ladies, and I am never sure that the ladies are really *ladies*. They speak French at me and laugh and say that I am "quaint." It is quite distressing.

Around midnight, I decided that I could not take any more. It was clear the merriment was just getting started, and in the garden there appeared to be a horrifying spontaneous play being performed, with the men dressed in women's clothing—and not much of it—and the five or so ladies laughing and applauding.

Catherine was in the midst of all of this revelry, and I could not bear it.

I went up to her and whispered in her ear that I was feeling quite ill, and she rose immediately. She is always so attentive to me, and I felt dreadful for lying to her, but I really did not like where the entertainment was headed. Catherine is so young! She does not think she is, but I am older than her by four years, and I cannot even begin to imagine Marianne being surrounded by these people.

We left immediately, and Catherine seemed as usual in the carriage. When I went to breakfast this morning, I assumed she was still asleep. But at some point in the afternoon, one of the chambermaids drew me aside and whispered that Catherine was still not home. Still not *home*? I panicked and rushed to her bedroom. It was empty, everything untouched, her clothes and shoes from last night still missing.

God help me, I then did something I should not have done. I told the maid very calmly that Catherine had gone to stay at the home of one of the ladies at the party and that she had only come home with me briefly to retrieve a few things. I do not know if she believed me, but she is a young thing, so perhaps she did.

What is worse is that I know exactly where she is. She is at the home of LaFrance. She must have snuck out again after coming home with me. This is the young man I caught her with some time ago—I believe I told you about it. They were in the garden in an embrace, and I was too shocked to intervene. I should have done something, I know I should have.

This LaFrance is not a bad person—he seems quite gentle and sweet, and he is an artist of some kind—but I need not tell you that this makes absolutely no difference! He is not an appropriate match for her at all. She is the daughter of an earl, and he is a poor émigré—and at any rate, she is not out!

Catherine would laugh at me for saying she is not out, as her papa has made sure she cannot be out by banishing her to Wansdyke. She has no way of even having a London Season. But there it is. I am not out, and neither is she, which means she cannot be running wild with LaFrance! This would be scandal on top of scandal!

I worry that the staff is gossiping, but there aren't many people here, fortunately. Claverton House is always empty, and I am the only person attending to Catherine besides that young chambermaid, who is much too innocent to conjure up an image of what is really happening. There is no butler, just a footman who does the job when absolutely necessary.

Catherine would not have found it difficult to slip out. The cook is the wife of the head groom; her meals when we are not entertaining are simple, and we normally send word downstairs when we wish to be served. Indeed, I just heard from her and was forced to tell her that we will both be out this evening.

Because there is no other choice—I must head to LaFrance's immediately. Oh, Booke, I am scared. I do not know what I will find!

Please keep me in your prayers.

I am always your affectionate friend,

Lydia

Chapter Thirty-Two

My dear Booke,

I am back. And Catherine came with me.

I am shaken and do not know what to do next.

LaFrance loves her, he says. He will never give her up. And Catherine believes that she is ever so happy and having so much fun. Her eyes were shining when I confronted her. She was in a state of undress that embarrassed me, lolling about in what appeared to be a borrowed dressing gown, but she was indifferent to my consternation.

She clearly did not spend the night in a guest bedroom.

I wonder if this was her first time with a man or whether I have been a fool and not seen what was in front of my face. There are so many things to worry about now. What if there is a child? Disease? Gossip and the ruin of her reputation? I did not realize these would be my worries when I agreed to live as Catherine's companion. I am horrified and frightened of what lies ahead.

I begged to speak to her in private, but she would not let LaFrance go. She told me that whatever I had to say could be said in front of him, so I gave up and told her that she needs to be mindful of her actions, her station—and she snapped at me horribly, dear Booke.

She is so deeply angry at all the people in her life who have hurt her, especially her father (who has no idea where she is and is indifferent to the point of being the most monstrous parental figure ever, beyond even Lady Durand, who at least tries her best for her own children). It has made her reckless about hurting herself. She retorted that I should not be telling her anything about her "station," since she is not able to take up her position in society as an earl's daughter anyway.

What was most hurtful was her shouting at me that I of all people should not speak to her this way, as I was merely the by-blow of a cruel and immoral duke who did not even give me what I was owed as his daughter. She screamed that she was almost as unfortunate as I and that I should understand her, given that we are both defective and cast aside for reasons beyond our control.

Of course she is right. What do I know of living as an earl's daughter? I have watched Lady Durand admonish her children to mind their station as children of a duke, but does that give me any authority on this subject?

I do not know, and perhaps Catherine was right to correct me. I do not think I feel her pain. I have always wanted an independent life, and I have always been sure that I could achieve it if I worked hard and craftily. The only confusing detail has been Lady Durand's effort to marry me off to Mr. Dryden, which I admit I still find perplexing. But Catherine cannot live independently because of her leg and because she cannot possibly work and earn her own money.

Who knows what fate lies ahead for her. When her father dies, his title will revert to the crown, and she will be a nobody. She may be a very wealthy nobody, but I do not think all the money in the world will cure her of her loneliness.

I am heartsick, my dear friend. This is my fault. I was too innocent and did not know how to take care of her. I should never have introduced her to LaFrance. I should never have allowed her to go to all those inappropriate gatherings. I should not have allowed her to slip away from me so easily. Friends are supposed to take care of each other, and I have failed miserably, even though she has been my savior.

LaFrance tried to calm her down. I do not think he is conniving or deceitful, but I do not know anything about men of his nationality or background. He seems to care for her, though he mostly appears to be dazzled by her beauty and vivacity, and on occasion I think he is a little afraid of her. If I had sensed even the smallest attempt to swindle her out of money or threaten her in any way, I would not have hesitated to drag her out of that house, even if she had screamed and hit me.

Sometimes I remember that Catherine is practically a child. Compared to her, I feel very old indeed, even though I am just nineteen. She might believe that she has grown up quickly and is very wise, especially now that she thinks she knows about love, but she is so young!

While we were at LaFrance's house, a friend of his arrived, and I was able to persuade Catherine that him finding her there in that state would mean her ruin. She laughed at me, but I think I saw a tinge of hesitation in her eyes. Despite her cynicism and anger, she knows that if she is shunned by London society, it will absolutely get back to her father and there will be consequences even graver than the ones she already faces. Fortunately, I was there to help her back into her clothes and redo her hair, so she looked entirely presentable by the time LaFrance's friend walked into the parlor, where we were pretending to sip tea.

This man, this friend of LaFrance—I do not like him at all. He looked Catherine up and down, then turned his gaze on me and seemed to be memorizing every curve of my face. I grew hot under his stare. LaFrance said he was a dealer of art and expensive furniture. He kept looking at Catherine and smirking, which made me wonder, because Catherine said she had never seen him before.

He spoke well and was nicely dressed, but something about him felt very strange. He wore a big gold signet ring, as if he were a lord, and I did not like his puce waistcoat. This may sound strange, but he was not a young man, yet he dressed like a young man of fashion. It was wrong in so many ways, but it is difficult for me to explain how.

Oh, Booke, I hate myself for introducing LaFrance to Catherine. I should have sent him packing when he came up to me and asked to meet her, but I had heard Catherine speaking French and thought perhaps she could assist him. I never thought it would come to this!

LaFrance's friend invited himself to a meal, and I managed to use this as an excuse for us to leave. He was clearly there for some purpose and eager for us to be gone. LaFrance kept stealing meaningful looks at Catherine, which I wish he had not! His friend saw every single one of them, I am sure. I am worried that he thought her dress was overly fancy for the hour, because of course it was her dress from the previous night. But Catherine had regained her composure by this point and was content to leave.

I have put her to bed and told more lies to the servants. I must figure out what to do about LaFrance, and possibly his friend. If he were to spread rumors, and if he understands how powerful

Catherine's family is, and if and if and if...terrible things could happen, and it would be my fault for not attending to her better.

I do not know what I would do if I could not unburden my heart to you, dearest friend. While I love and esteem Catherine and deeply appreciate her innate kindness to me, I know that in this harsh world, you are really the only one I can trust absolutely.

Your devoted friend, most affectionately yours,

Lydia

Chapter Thirty-Three

Dear Booke,

Since that horrible day, Catherine has told me all. Back at Claverton House, surrounded by the trappings of wealth and power, she seems to understand that what she has done was exceedingly foolish. Some of what she said, I cannot tell you. I cannot write those words on these pages; even now I blush and grow agitated at the thought of the antics she participated in.

But never mind that. The critical thing is that THERE IS A PORTRAIT. A portrait of Catherine—a compromising portrait. It is not finished, she tells me, but she has sat for LaFrance unclothed a number of times. She swears that she thought she was in love with him, that her money would take care of them both. However, when I pointed out that her money is HER FATHER'S MONEY, she grew pale. It had not quite occurred to her that her father has not actually been as drastic as he has the power to be. He could bar her from Wansdyke, cut off her bank account, dismiss her loyal staff, and guarantee that no one speaks to her ever again.

I was ill with anxiety after she told me about the portrait. I could not think of what to do. She no longer has dreams of marrying LaFrance. She knows they cannot live on his art, and she also knows that if anyone finds out about their affair, someone will tell her father.

I cannot believe what I just wrote. Was there ever anything so dreadful? I do not know how Catherine found herself in this predicament. She is so young and so damaged from her lack of love. Even I do not know what that must feel like, despite my own terrible circumstances.

I do not know if there is any way out of this.

Please help me, dear Booke. Please give me spiritual guidance and the peace of mind to think my way out of this terrible situation, to devise some way of saving Catherine. She only wished to help me and has been so generous with me. If we could go back to the way we were at Wansdyke, I could spend my entire life free from worry in exchange for being her loyal friend. This is all I want, to be free and free from worry.

Perhaps an idea will float into my head at exactly the right moment, and if it does, I will know that you are out there somewhere, always thinking of me as I think of you.

I am always your friend,

Lydia

Chapter Thirty-Four

My dearest Booke,

Yesterday, Catherine admitted that her feelings for LaFrance had cooled and that she now saw the error of her ways. After her last meeting with him, he sent her several notes, begging to see her, which she has not answered.

I was very relieved, but also nervous. What if he does something rash? And this portrait...what would happen to the portrait?

Catherine seemed unconcerned about the portrait. She said that LaFrance fancied himself a true artist and that he wanted to paint her portrait because he was experimenting with some particular perspective. She scoffed that he would not be interested in black-mail, that it wasn't in his nature to stoop to such a level.

I was more concerned with his foppish, foolish friends than with LaFrance himself. I worried they might convince him to do something that he otherwise would not.

That man who had come to visit him when we were there...I did not like him. I wished I knew his name, but of course we had not been introduced. I remembered his big gold signet ring and his puce waistcoat, and I remembered that he was a little paunchy and ruddy-faced and affected youth—and perhaps status—although he was not young. Something about him had seemed false and deceitful, but I could not put my finger on it.

Finally, I decided that I needed to speak to LaFrance myself. There was no way around this but to tell him that his affair with Catherine was over. And I thought perhaps I could get him to tell me if anyone knew about that portrait.

I set out to call on LaFrance alone. It was of course highly improper for me to visit him on my own, but what could I do? I was certainly not going to bring Catherine along!

Catherine had been invited to a boring little evening card party of the sort she normally disdained, but she seemed chastened and a bit mortified after her escapades with LaFrance and his friends and was quite happy to attend. I escorted her to the party, but I was not included in the card games, of course, so I told Catherine and the hostess that I wanted to retrieve a warmer cloak and change my gloves, and then I slipped out of the house.

I was in luck—LaFrance was at home alone. He had been drinking, I could see, and I instantly regretted having handed my cloak and hat to the footman when I came in, as I thought I might need to beat a hasty retreat if he was very intoxicated. I soon saw that he was sad, not angry, and when he looked up and saw me, his entire countenance bloomed with so much love and hope that I almost felt guilty.

"She is not with me," I said quickly. His face fell, and he gestured toward a chair across the room before putting his head in his hands. He was unshaven and unkempt, as if he had not changed his clothes since we had seen him several days before. An untouched tray of food was abandoned on a small table nearby.

I let the silence fill the room for a moment, not quite knowing how to begin. But when I opened my mouth to launch into the speech I had rehearsed on the way, he gave a great sigh and muttered, "She is not coming back."

"No," I said, greatly relieved that I was spared having to recite my prepared speech.

"I thought she loved me. She said she loved me..." he said, but I detected a note of his shame in his voice. I could not explain, of course, that Catherine was ill-equipped to love anyone at all, given her lack of experience with the emotion, but I felt sorry for him nonetheless.

"She is young," is what I finally said, as gently as I could. LaFrance shrugged and downed his drink. He lifted the bottle and offered it to me, but I shook my head. I did not want my mind to be fuzzy in the event that I needed to leave quickly.

As he poured another glass of the stuff for himself, I looked around the parlor rather anxiously, thinking that perhaps the portrait might be visible, but there was nothing but a sketch of a ballet dancer. It looked dusty, as if it were quite old.

He saw me looking at it and said, "That is not mine. This is a rented accommodation, you know. I do my work in the shed."

"I beg your pardon, did you say the shed?"

He nodded, downed his drink, and stood up. "Would you like to see it?"

I gasped. "No—no, thank you." I had no desire to see the portrait itself! I knew that I ought to look, but the thought of actually seeing the thing...I did not have the stomach for it. I had asked Catherine if it looked like her at all, and she had said very proudly —foolish girl—that it did indeed. She had said she trusted

LaFrance, and I'd never thought of him as evil or deceitful. But perhaps that was naïve of both of us.

"Then why are you here?" His speech was slurred, but his eyes were bright, and I was quite sure he was not as drunk as he sounded. "Are you not here to throw that wretched portrait into the fire?" He flung his glass at the fireplace, where it shattered into a million shards. I gave a little cry and shrank into my seat.

"It is not finished," he said glumly. "It is not finished, and perhaps it never will be. I will never see Catherine again."

"I am so sorry," I said, and meant it, but the shattered glass had frightened me, and I was wondering if I should leave. Had I said what I meant to say? Was it enough? Would he stop writing letters and leave Catherine alone now? Could I rely on him to stop working on that portrait? And had he told anyone else about it?

As I was running these questions through my mind, you will not believe who walked into the room. It was that man, the one who had been there when Catherine and I were there last.

"Stevenson!" LaFrance seemed equally startled to see him. "I did not expect you tonight."

"I had not planned on coming," said Stevenson. He was looking around the room as if searching for something, and then his gaze fastened on me. I bowed slightly, trying to keep my countenance bland, but unlike the last time, he was not trying to be polite. He stared at me with a hostile expression.

"You," he said. "Who are you? Lady Catherine's friend, I presume."

I bristled, for I did not see why he needed to know my name. In fact, I was dismayed that he knew who Catherine was, although of course he must have asked LaFrance after we'd left the last time. I did not like the fact that we had not been introduced by someone I trusted, so I merely nodded, and then LaFrance came to my rescue. He seemed quite agitated.

"Stevenson, we agreed on a fortnight for those bills."

Bills! I caught myself before I let out a gasp. There was a swagger to this Stevenson person; it must've been what had set me off when I had first seen him. He was feeling powerful, apparently—and if LaFrance owed him money, that made a great deal of sense.

LaFrance glanced at me quickly, the shame on his countenance telling me my conjecture was correct. He was in debt to this disreputable poser.

"The situation has changed." Stevenson spoke loudly, his voice echoing off the walls as if he were giving a speech. Again, I got the distinct sense that he was playing a part, trying to be more refined than he really was.

"But my situation has also changed," LaFrance pleaded. "I am not able to paint. There have been some...developments. I need time."

"You have had plenty of time! I need that portrait!"

What portrait? I looked at LaFrance, who would not meet my gaze.

"You cannot have it. It is not finished. I may never finish it."

"Without it, I will not be able to get you the commissions you desire. There are many who wish to hire you, but I need to show them a serious painting. That portrait would get you the sort of patrons who would solve all your problems."

A horrible, cold feeling was creeping down my neck, down my spine. They were talking about the portrait of Catherine. Stevenson wanted to show it around London to persuade rich men to hire LaFrance. And he would certainly help himself to a fat commission.

"I told you, no," LaFrance was saying. He sounded firm, no longer drunk. He stared hard at Stevenson, but the man was not intimidated. Indeed, he walked casually over to the fireplace, where he turned his back on the room and warmed his hands.

LaFrance looked at me with much meaning but said nothing. I knew there was danger ahead. I wished this Stevenson man would leave, but he was clearly settling in for the evening, and I suspected he would push and push until LaFrance could resist no longer. I needed to do something, and fast. But what could I do? I could not handle Stevenson on my own, and even if LaFrance managed to get rid of him tonight, he would be back.

I felt desperate, but I needed to return to that cursed card party. I nodded to LaFrance and made my way to the door. He called for the footman to bring my wrap and my hat.

As I stood in the hall donning my cloak, LaFrance whispered to me that I should not worry, that he would never do anything to hurt Catherine. "I will send him away," he whispered, nodding in the direction of the parlor. "None of my work is in this house; there is no way for him to take it."

"He will not give up," I whispered back. I saw the fear in LaFrance's eyes and knew I was right, even though he tried to shrug it off.

I left the house in a hurry and arrived back at the card party without a new cloak or gloves, but no one noticed. It occurred to me that as I was merely Catherine's companion, no one was interested in my attire!

Catherine had forgotten I had ever left and was squealing with glee because she kept winning her hands. I, however, was sick to my stomach. Dear Booke, I do not know what to do. I will be up all night trying to think. I know you are shaking your head at the trouble I get myself into. I know you think I should have married

Mr. Dryden after all. I am sure everyone under the sun would think so. I remain devoted to Catherine, but I am quite exhausted.

And I remain ever devoted to you, my bosom friend.

I am ever your most affectionate,

Lydia

Chapter Thirty-Five

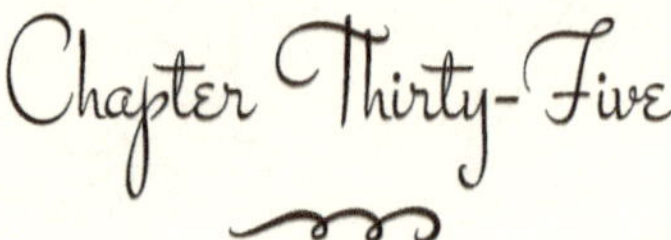

BELOVED FRIEND,

I could not think of any other solution to Catherine's troubles, so I composed a letter to Mr. Dryden. Yes, Mr. Dryden! I think only he can save Catherine now.

Catherine received a note from LaFrance. Stevenson, that snake, has seen the unfinished portrait—which is apparently finished enough that Catherine is unmistakably recognizable. And while he has not wrested it away from LaFrance, he is prepared to tell his connections about it in hopes that it will generate commissions, from which he will earn a tidy profit.

This cannot happen!

I am going to plead with Mr. Dryden to help me. At one time he was willing to marry me. I have his ring. He is an honorable man, I know it. I will offer myself to him in exchange for help for Catherine.

I know this seems insane. But I think I have been wrong-headed about the situation all along.

Men, and only men, have power in this world. I know this, and you know this, and Catherine knows this. Who was I to think that Catherine could have a liaison with a man and not be harmed? It's ridiculous that I even tried to speak to LaFrance. As a lowly female, I had no possible way to persuade him to give me the portrait or to destroy it. Only Stevenson, a MAN, could do that.

Catherine has quite a lot of money, but I suspect that if she were to offer a sum to LaFrance for the portrait, he would refuse. Why? Because he is a MAN, and all he wants from her is that which only a woman can give him. Money isn't interesting if he gets it from a woman. Ultimately, men feel powerful and pleased with themselves when they are dominating a female. It delights them more than money ever could. It is disgusting.

And this is what made me realize that the only solution to this problem is to use the weapon I have not tried to use until now. I am a female, and I have something to offer Mr. Dryden, who is a man of wealth and power. I can give up my independence and offer myself to him in order to repair Catherine's error.

You wonder what exactly I want him to do, dear Booke? I want him to go to LaFrance and to either buy that portrait or make LaFrance destroy it. If he will not, then I want him to prevent that odious Mr. Stevenson from getting his hands on it and showing it all around town. With money and threats, perhaps it can be accomplished. And I know Mr. Dryden will have money, as Lady Durand paid him to marry me.

It is a world of men, dear Booke. I cannot do anything or make anyone do anything, but Mr. Dryden is a man, so he can do these things. I am operating under the assumption that he still wants to marry me and was disappointed when I said no. If he will help Catherine by getting rid of this portrait, I will marry him.

This scheme sounds absurd, I know. What if Mr. Dryden is not honorable? What if he gossips and spreads rumors? What if he declares that Catherine deserves whatever fate lies in wait for her? What if all of Marianne's panicked conjectures are true, and Mr. Dryden is hiding some kind of strange secret?

But I must help Catherine. She helped me to get out of the clutches of Lady Durand when I had no other options. I cannot stand by and watch this tragedy play out on the stage that is London. It would mean ruin for her forever.

Poor Catherine. She is so young. She acts as if she is so wise, but she does not know how the world will treat her once that painting has been seen. She claims to know what society is like, but because she has never spent much time among her equals, she doesn't know what it will be like to be shunned and shamed, pointed at on the streets, unable to attend any functions and invited nowhere. I don't want that for her.

And I know that if I marry Mr. Dryden I will have to leave her, but when I weigh this against her certain ruin, possibly forever...I do not think I have a choice. While I know that she did not hire me to protect her (she would have laughed at such a thought), I feel as if I have failed my friend. If I can fix this misstep, I will consider that I have made at least partial amends.

I took the letter to Mr. Dryden's rented apartments myself, despite my fears that I would look quite disreputable. He was not at home, and the maid who answered the door was pleasant and cheerful, which was fortunate. She did not seem to think ill of me for coming alone on such an errand, and indeed she invited me in to wait. She said that he was at his doctor's, which caused me some concern. He did say he was a bit unwell in one of his letters (so long ago!), but he did not say anything about doctors. I hope he is not ill.

I was too scared to wait, so I declined and was walking away from the building when I heard a shout. It was he, running down the street to stop me. He looked a bit ridiculous with his dusty brown coat flapping as he ran, surrounded by staring strangers who were obviously appalled at his lack of decorum. I was so relieved to see him, however, that I nearly burst into tears. He has such a kind, interested face.

When he reached me, I swear I could have reached out to grasp his hands, I was so overcome! I settled on gripping my reticule so tightly that I later discovered I had bent you—my current pocket book!—into a wrinkled leather roll.

He asked how he could be of service, but we were standing in the middle of the street with people all around us, so I asked if he would walk with me. I knew there was a little row of shops nearby, and I thought perhaps we could glance into the windows and look quite inconspicuous that way.

He asked if I would not rather come into the house, but I was afraid of more eyes upon us, so he agreed to walk with me. Of course, in such a setting I could not give any details. I could not bring myself to shame Catherine in the letter I'd written him, and now I found I could not shame her in speech, either.

Instead, I stood very straight with my shoulders back and looked directly into his eyes and stated boldly that if he would still have me, I would be honored to accept his previous proposal.

He was shocked. I could see the confusion and dismay written all over his face, though he tried to hide it.

Booke, I was never so mortified in my life. If I could have turned around and fled, I believe I would have! But of course, I had to stand there and stare confidently back at him.

His expression got softer as he gazed at me. My heart gave a great thump, and I was awash in regret at my previous refusal of his offer. Catherine had persuaded me not to trust him. She had told me that men were worthless, that marriage was a trap. And she was not wrong. Now she is in trouble because she trusted a man, and to get her out of this predicament, I would have to trust a man.

Something about this parallel struck me as both funny and dreadful, and tears came to my eyes. I hurriedly searched in my reticule for a handkerchief—yes, one of my lovely embroidered handkerchiefs that not too long ago was commanding a nice amount in the Bath shops!

He asked very gently if anything had happened to cause this change of heart. I was ready for this question. I had planned to tell him a carefully edited story, but now that the moment had come, I could not speak. Instead, I struggled to hold back more tears. This kind man whom I had treated so poorly—even to the point of keeping that lovely ring, which I should never have accepted—was the only one who could right Catherine's dreadful mistake, and he owed me nothing. Why would he help Catherine?

"You are upset," he said when I buried my face in my handkerchief and turned away. "I will do anything, anything at all, to take your burdens away. Please tell me what I can do for you. Is it Lady Durand? Does she treat you badly?"

At this I lifted my head, surprised that he would ask such a thing. I did not think anyone in the world besides me knew what a viper Lady Durand was. I also did not realize until that moment that he did not realize I was now in Catherine's employ.

"I—I am no longer in Lady Durand's household," I managed to say. "She has cast me out."

"Cast you out?" Mr. Dryden seemed even more shocked than before. He raised his voice. "How did this happen?"

I could not help it—I launched into a rambling explanation of Lady Durand's anger over my refusal of his proposal and told him I had been saved by my friend, Lady Catherine. I explained that I was Catherine's companion and that certain things had occurred that presented a risk to her reputation—and, I added, possibly to mine. That was an embellishment, as I have no particular reputation to protect, but I thought it might prepare Mr. Dryden to hear my request, as what I was asking was sure to horrify him.

"Do you mean to say that refusing my offer has resulted in—" He seemed unable to say the words. He shook his head. "So in a sense, this is all *my* fault."

I was aghast. "No! No, Mr. Dryden, my current situation is not your fault. Please do not—"

"But you say you have been cast out of the household in which you grew up because you did not want this marriage."

"Yes, that much is true, but—"

"Then it comes back to me, and I am responsible." Mr. Dryden went silent for a moment, and I was afraid to say anything more. It was not his fault. I did not want to marry, and that was my fault, and Lady Durand was evil, and that was her fault. The inside of my head felt confused, as if I were wading through treacle.

Eventually, Mr. Dryden gave a great sigh. "It is too late." His expression was sorrowful, and I felt my stomach turn to ice and the color drain from my face.

He turned to me and reached out to grasp my hands in his. "I know this is not something I should say, but...I was quite disappointed that you declined my offer. I hoped that perhaps I could meet you again and persuade you—especially after you said you had come to London—but alas, I could not convince you to meet with me. Now that you are willing to reconsider, I am sad to say it is too late. I have been promised to another."

I nodded numbly. Of course! Why should I think that he would still be available or interested? I did not expect my heart to sink quite the way it did, though. It felt as if the sun had stopped shining, as if nothing would be happy ever again.

"But I will help you," he continued, "because I feel some level of responsibility in this situation. And also because"—here he gripped my hands even more tightly—"I still admire you. You are strong, and a loyal friend. I would have liked such a friend by my side."

He dropped my hands. "We will go back to my apartments, and you will tell me all. And I will try to solve whatever problem your friend Lady Catherine has got herself into."

I was so ashamed. I had been ready to marry him, even though it was against my better judgment. And in this strange twist, I wouldn't be able to marry him, but he was still going to help me. I did not deserve this!

For a moment, I stood, unable to move, as I could not bear the thought of sitting in his parlor with the shame of my callous behavior hanging over me like a storm cloud. But then he saw my face, and his entire demeanor softened with kindness.

Dear, dear Booke! I never knew that some people are just GOOD people. Some people, like Marianne, are kind and generous, but they live in a state of constant anxiety because they are surrounded by bad things. Marianne runs and hides at the least bit of conflict, so I cannot depend on her.

Meanwhile, Catherine is strong, but she shows me a bitter, angry, vengeful side from time to time. I thought that all humanity was as scarred and doomed to sadness and despair as I was, as Catherine was, as Lady Durand clearly is. Everywhere I look, I see people doing terrible things because they are in pain. They seek to inflict their pain on others in order to save themselves.

But Mr. Dryden has never done me any harm, and as far as I can tell, he simply has no bad feelings in him. He is a farmer, is not particularly handsome, and wears unfashionable, dusty clothes. But on this gloomy day on this London street, he looked like an angel to me.

After a cup of hot, bitter tea, I was able to tell him the story—the whole story, starting with who I am, who I have turned out to be, and why I am loyal to Catherine. I explained why I declined his proposal, trying not to flinch as I told him that I was afraid to trust him because of Lady Durand.

I also explained that I would gladly marry him—not merely to save Catherine, but also because I know he is a good person. At this, he shook his head sadly and held up a hand, so I did not continue in that vein.

I will readily admit that at first I lied about the exact nature of Catherine's missteps. I simply could not bring myself to tell the full story aloud and hoped he might read into my faltering speech the truth of what had transpired. I told him that Catherine had entered into an "improper" relationship with an artist. I also told him that there appeared to be "a sketch or two" that documented their relationship. I tried not to dwell on this but hoped he would see my lie for what it was.

To his credit, Mr. Dryden stopped me immediately and asked what I meant. He is no fool, and of course he is far older than I and must know much more about the sordid corners of society. There was a stricken look in his eyes—knowing that LaFrance was an artist and that Catherine had made some foolish decisions was clearly enough for him to understand what had occurred. He said quietly, "Am I to understand that there is a painting of Lady Catherine?"

In that moment I felt the heavy burden of how I had failed her, and a fresh wave of guilt and fear washed over me. As her paid companion, her chaperone, and her friend, I needed to do more than coyly dance around the subject. I needed to get the words out so I could save her. I needed to be a grown woman, not a meek, shy child, especially since I was offering to be his wife. And I needed to be responsible and mature if I wanted to save Catherine.

"Yes," I managed to say. "There is an incriminating portrait. I have not seen it, but Lady Catherine told me that she is...she is... unclothed, and that the likeness is unmistakable."

"Good God," Mr. Dryden said softly.

"If this portrait is shown widely," I continued, "Lady Catherine will be ruined. LaFrance's friend has already seen it, so there is at least one person who knows her secret."

When I explained that Stevenson had found out about the liaison and wanted to use it to gain personal advantage, Mr. Dryden's face darkened, and he seemed to bite his tongue several times in order to keep himself from exclaiming. With just the briefest explanation of Stevenson's goal—to use the relationship with Catherine to sell LaFrance's services, for which he would collect a fee—Mr. Dryden understood what I was saying. At least, I believe so.

Mr. Dryden assured me he would do all he could to help, and I returned home full of both hope and worry. He is my only prayer, and if he cannot save Catherine, no one can.

I am saddened that there is nothing I can do for Mr. Dryden that will make him happy. He seemed very low in spirit. I worry that he is ill, perhaps extremely ill, and that he has extended his stay in London for the purpose of seeing various doctors. I truly would marry him—I would be glad to marry him—but I did not bring up the subject again. I suppose it is for the best that I remain devoted to Catherine.

Please pray for an easy end to all of this disorder. I am deeply grateful for your patient ear, my dear Booke.

I remain yours truly and affectionately,

Lydia

Chapter Thirty-Six

My dearest,

If I am dragged away to prison, let this be a record of all that that has transpired. Dear Lord, I never thought that in my effort to do right by Catherine, I would find myself in such a terrible situation.

I swear that I did not mean to do it. I swear on all that is good and true, I did not mean to do it, and I regret it. I am sorry and shall repent forevermore...

I have stared at the above words for a long time, and in the end, I cannot lie to you. I thought I might write words that would absolve me of my crime and that anyone who finds this book might read it and know that I am not a bad person, or an evil person, or insane.

But perhaps I really am a bad person, because in truth I do not feel the least bit of regret for what I have done.

Yesterday, Mr. Dryden sent me a note saying he wished to call and that I could expect him early. I immediately gave the servants the day off and asked the cook to leave us a light repast for today.

I knew that Catherine was invited to an event in the evening and would be having supper there. I just did not want the servants to look askance at poor Mr. Dryden and his dusty brown coat and unpolished boots. I also feared that we would have to spend a long time alone in the library, and even though we have very limited staff here at Claverton House, I feared the housekeeper's haughty stare and the impertinent grin of the second footman.

When the knocker sounded, I hurried to answer the door myself and was shocked to see not Mr. Dryden but LaFrance's friend Stevenson.

He pushed his way in before I could react, then whirled around and demanded to see Catherine.

"I beg your pardon?" was all I could stammer.

"I wish to see your mistress," he said in an imperious tone. Once again, he was affecting that loud, echoing voice, like an actor on a stage. He wore a driving coat with many capes, as if he were a young man of fashion, which looked decidedly odd on a middle-aged man with a sizable belly. He removed his hat, placed it on the table beside him, and leaned his obnoxious ivory-headed walking cane against the wall next to it.

"She is not at home," I said finally. "How may I—"

"I know she is at home," he interrupted, "because she does not go out without you. If you are at home, she is at home."

I wrinkled my brow. He clearly thought Catherine's limp was more of a burden than it actually was. It was in my moment of hesitation that disaster occurred. Stevenson turned to survey the staircase that headed upstairs to the bedrooms, and I panicked, thinking that he meant to storm into Catherine's bedroom. After all, if he knew about the portrait, he must think her a very loose woman indeed, perhaps someone who would not mind entertaining strange gentlemen in her boudoir.

"Stop!" I cried as he seemed to start for the stairs. He turned and, upon seeing my face, began to laugh.

"What, do you mean to protect your mistress's virtue? Young lady, I admire your dedication, but it is too late for that!"

At this moment, the worst possible moment, Catherine appeared at the top of the stairs. She was en déshabillé (that foolish girl, what on earth was she thinking?) with her hair mussed, her face tired. She had clearly just gotten out of bed, prepared to yell at me for causing a disturbance too early in the day. She paused, frowning down at us in confusion.

"Who is at the door?"

I wish with all my might that she had not spoken, for Stevenson looked swiftly toward the stairs, and my blood ran cold. Could I stop him from going upstairs? Could two petite women overpower a thickset man?

"Ah! Lady Catherine!" Stevenson's voice brimmed with amusement, and his words caused my ears to roar, my head to fill with screams of danger. He turned to smirk at me, then began to stride toward the stairs. I shouted at him to stop, while Catherine instinctively took a step backward.

"I just want to see your dressing room," he said in a joking tone. "I am sure that you will not prevent me? I know your staff is not at home, for I spoke to one of your young chambermaids as she left earlier. Very helpful—she said that everyone was given a holiday today. I am here with a very profitable business offer—I am sure you will not mind if I intrude upon your morning. Your servant girl can bring us some coffee, perhaps?" He smirked in my direction, and I understood that I was the "servant girl" in question.

I cannot explain to you the workings of my mind; I am sure there was some flow of logic, but the moment flashed by so quickly that I did not have time to reflect. For the next thing I knew, I was holding the walking cane Stevenson had leant against the wall—it was made of ebony and some kind of hard white material, perhaps ivory or whalebone, and had a substantial crook at the top. I had thought it a ridiculous and pretentious accessory to his ridiculous and pretentious many-caped topcoat, but in my moment of need, I grabbed it and leapt up the stairs behind him.

I hooked the crook of the cane into the neck of his stupid coat and pulled with all my strength.

He tumbled backward down the stairs, but instead of falling on top of me as I had expected, he somersaulted past and slammed his head into the bannister where it connected to the floor. As I gazed down in horror, blood flowed from his broken skull onto the white marble, pooling slowly and seeping into his carefully coiffed blond hair.

Catherine stood frozen at the top of the stairs, her hand over the mouth, her eyes shocked. After a moment, she grasped the bannister as if she might swoon.

Oh, Booke. I had meant to stop him, not to kill him.

Well.

Honestly speaking, I do not think the world will suffer without him.

Perhaps there is something truly wrong with me, for while I was horrified by what I had done, I was not horrified by the result. That is not normal, I fear. But then, I have always known there was some broken part of me deep inside, where I did not feel the angst and sorrow about my situation that I should have felt. Lady

Durand did not inspire tears, just anger. My papa did not inspire sadness, just disgust.

I do not have that deep well of sorrow in me that Catherine has. Perhaps I am inhuman, a monster without compassion or feeling. Stevenson lay on the floor, almost certainly dead, and I did not feel at all sorry for him. I was only sorry for myself because I might end up in prison.

I must stop, I hear voices. I am writing this quickly, just in case I am taken away. But there is more to this story.

Darling Booke, I am ever yours.

Chapter Thirty-Seven

MOST BELOVED FRIEND,

I am sorry I left you without finishing the tale of that dreadful day! I had written so much, my wrist hurt, and I heard gossiping in the hall, so I felt compelled to listen. I was worried that the servants had found remains of Stevenson's blood on the staircase or the bannister, but they were merely gossiping about minor things, so I have come back in to finish the story for you.

Catherine let out a cry when she saw all the blood, but I must commend her for her composure. She did not swoon or panic but descended the stairs to get a better view.

"Is he dead?" she whispered.

"Most certainly," I replied. I went to where the body lay and prodded it with my toe. Catherine gave a gasp.

"What shall we do?"

"It was an accident," I said. "I was trying to stop him from going upstairs. He might have attacked you."

"Lydia, if my father hears about this—"

"I know," I interrupted. I did not want to think about her father. I was thinking about my own father! What would happen if Papa were to hear that I had killed a man? What would Lady Durand say? What effect would this have on the family? Would they simply deny that I was part of the family?

I thought of Jonathan Barrow, that poor man. I do not remember him at all and have no idea what sort of person he is, other than the savior who agreed to spare me the label of "bastard." Had I just ruined his life? And what about my mother? Would she finally succeed in jumping out a window, all because I had stopped Stevenson from racing upstairs to do who knew what to Catherine?

At that moment, there was a quiet knock at the door, and Catherine and I both jumped. We looked at each other fearfully. I did not feel the least bit bad that Stevenson was dead, but I did not want to go to prison. What would Catherine do without me? I was the only one who knew her secret and could protect her. I did not think LaFrance intended to do her harm, and Stevenson would no longer cause her any trouble, but what if someone saw that half-finished portrait someday and identified her?

I hurried into the parlor and peeked out the window. My heart swelled with relief—it was Mr. Dryden. Then I realized—Mr. Dryden! Good God, I had forgotten! The whole point of emptying the house of servants had been to allow Mr. Dryden to visit in private. He had agreed to help me save Catherine! But now, what to do?

I stood very still, grasping the window frame until I could feel the wood biting into my fingertips and the skin of my palms. This was the moment of reckoning. I had trusted Mr. Dryden with Catherine's secret—most of it, anyway—but this! It was one thing to ask him to dispose of a portrait and to bribe or threaten Stevenson; it was another to invite him into a house where a dead body lay bleeding upon the floor.

I had to make a decision, and dear Booke, you know that I act on instinct more than I want to admit. I decided to trust him. I can say that I had no choice, but that's not really true. I did have a choice, and I chose trust. I trusted Mr. Dryden.

I dashed over to the door and opened it a crack. "I am so sorry," I whispered, "but there has been a—a—mishap. Are you alone?"

"I am alone," he replied, and I opened the door just enough to let him in.

He stood for a moment, taking in the horrible scene in the entry-way. After a moment, he raised his eyes to look at Catherine, who stood in her dressing gown halfway up the stairs.

"Lady Catherine, if you would, please go back upstairs," I said. She turned and obeyed without a word.

"It was an accident," I said to Mr. Dryden, who had turned his gaze back to the body on the floor. "He was charging up the stairs toward Lady Catherine, and I—I pulled him back with that cane." I pointed at the cane, lying abandoned to one side of the staircase. "That is Mr. Stevenson," I added, realizing that he had no idea who the victim was. "He was here to...well, I assume he was here to blackmail her."

At this, Mr. Dryden's eyes narrowed, but he remained silent. I wondered if I should explain further, but my throat felt so dry, I think I would have choked on the words. There was a very long silence, during which I could hear the sounds of early-morning London outside: birds chirping, snatches of laughter and conversa-tion, clip-clops from the carriage horses of our wealthy neighbors. It seemed peaceful and happy and surreal.

When he finally spoke, Mr. Dryden was grim. "I will take care of this," he said.

"But what shall I do? How can I help?" I asked. I was panicked, as I wondered how we could possibly dispose of a body as big and lumpy as Stevenson's.

"You were not here," he said.

"I was not here?" I demanded, confused. "I certainly was!"

"No, you were not here. You were upstairs with Lady Catherine. I entered the house, saw this man ascending the stairs, demanded that he stop, and when he did not, I pulled him down with that walking cane," he added, nodding at the cane. He turned to me and said apologetically, "It will require that I tell another small lie as well. I apologize in advance for this, but it is the best way."

"What do you mean?"

Mr. Dryden heaved a sigh. He reached out and took both my hands in his. I was too shocked to protest—and indeed, I don't believe I wanted to protest, Booke! His hands were warm, and mine were cold, and I feel as if the kindness that permeates his entire being were flowing into my body and warming my heart.

"Listen to me, my dear. The simplest thing would be for you and Lady Catherine not to have seen what transpired. I will tell the constable that I was the only witness and that I had never seen this man in my life, which is true, but that he was threatening you as he charged up the stairs. You and Lady Catherine will not be involved. I can pay the constable to keep the inquest quiet. If the man's family demands a more thorough explanation, I will pay them. I doubt they will want to make this incident public. I am sure I can buy their silence."

"You cannot!" I gasped, but Mr. Dryden squeezed my hands tight and continued.

"I said there would be another small lie. No one will find out about the lie, but it will satisfy my own heart's desire. I will say that you and I were involved in a liaison and that I was here to pursue it. That will explain why I was here and why you have dismissed your help for the day."

"Mr. Dryden—"

"Let me finish, Lydia, please!" He looked miserable, so I stopped speaking. "I am happy to do this for you. An inquest is a tiresome ordeal. You will not like having to deal with the constable, and it will be impossible to keep people from gossiping if it becomes known that Lady Catherine was involved. It is easiest if we just say that I was the one who committed this act of unintentional violence." He looked down at Stevenson's sprawled form. "Is this the man you mentioned to me? The one who was making threats against Lady Catherine?"

"Yes," I whispered. "Mr. Dryden, you are too good to me. I do not deserve—"

"No, Lydia, I am the one who does not deserve you. You were right to turn down my offer. I am too ashamed to tell you the whole of it now, but one day I will write to you and explain everything so that I do not have to look you in the eye as I speak. I hope you do not mind that I call you by your Christian name? You are so beautiful, and your name is so beautiful. I do not want to call you Miss Barrow any longer." He gave a brief smile. "And now, let me go for the constable. I will bring him in through the back door, if you will show me where it is. Unfortunately, we have to leave the body be until he sees it so that he can confirm my story."

And that, dear Booke, is what happened. We had to leave Stevenson on the floor until the constable arrived with two sturdy helpers. He took notes and interviewed both Catherine and myself, but as we stuck to the story Mr. Dryden had concocted, the interviews were brief. We said we had seen and heard nothing until the incident itself. I was forced to say that Mr. Dryden and I were involved in a liaison, but the constable did not seem inclined to pursue that detail, fortunately.

It is incredible how a man with money can be so sure of his command over everything in his sight...and be absolutely correct. For Mr. Dryden was right—this warped story seemed to be of little interest to the constable, except insofar as it might lead to scandal for Catherine's father, the earl. The constable seemed eager to avoid any hostile interactions with the family, and the rough young women who were brought in to clean the hall were very happy to be overpaid for their services. From their speech, I could tell that they were not from this part of London, so I did not worry that they would gossip with the servants when they returned.

My dearest friend, I have such conflicted feelings about Mr. Dryden. I wonder what strange secret he was referring to when he said he did not deserve me. I wonder at the warm feeling I had when he called me by my Christian name. I am more determined than ever to stay by Catherine's side, but I am also bitterly disappointed that I may never again see this fine man.

Catherine is sure that he loves me, but she saw him only for the briefest moment before I sent her upstairs. She can know nothing of what he feels. I, however, wonder if he does love me. If so, I am wretched. Was I so close to happiness? Did I really turn away from that happiness? Is it possible that I have made him unhappy?

Catherine is such a child. I can see how little she knows of the world, even though she believes she is more sophisticated than I am. I am cautious and always thinking about propriety, but this is not because I agree with society's rules. Heavens, no. Why would I defend the rules that have had such a negative effect on my life?

No, I do not defend them, but I must protect myself against them, and Catherine needs me to protect her as well. She does not seem to realize that even the daughter of an earl can be ruined by not respecting the rules. When I turned down Mr. Dryden, it was because Catherine offered to protect me. But now I see that there is much I can do to protect her, too.

Was it the right thing, turning down Mr. Dryden? If I leave Catherine, what would happen to her? She would be stuck at Wansdyke forever, I imagine. Or she would get herself into some kind of terrible trouble.

I do not want to know the answers to all of my questions, dear Booke. I wish we could leave London and never come back.

Yours faithfully,

Lydia

Chapter Thirty-Eight

Dᴇᴀʀᴇꜱᴛ ᴏɴᴇ,

It has been a few days since the horrible event. I am exhausted. Catherine is exhausted. Neither of us speaks of what happened. Mr. Dryden sent a note to say that he had "taken care of everything" and we were not to worry, but of course we are worried.

It is just as well that we do not reside in London. At the moment, I long for Bath. I never thought I would feel this way, but I have now been completely ejected from the Durand family and have nowhere to go. Bath is all I have, and Wansdyke is my home so long as Catherine views it as home.

LaFrance sent a note, pleading with Catherine once more. He claimed to love her desperately and said that he was sick at heart because of her cold refusal to speak to him. I took charge this time, which I suppose I should have done from the start. I wrote back and said in the strongest possible language that he would not be seeing Catherine again. He then begged permission to call on us at Claverton House, which I denied. But the more I thought about it, the more nervous I became. Perhaps he had some specific piece of information to tell us? Something we needed to know regarding Stevenson?

In the end, I could not tolerate my own anxiety. I decided to pay a visit to LaFrance.

It was afternoon, and I could see the shabbiness of the furnishings and draperies clearly in the daylight. The part of London where he is staying is not disreputable, exactly, but I have become quite used to the environs of Claverton House, which is filled with fancy homes. LaFrance's is a different sort of neighborhood, filled with émigrés in rented accommodations.

LaFrance answered the door himself and did not seem surprised to see me. He let me into the hall without a word and beckoned me to follow him. To my surprise, he walked past the parlor and kept going. I suddenly realized what was happening. He was taking me to the shed where he worked.

I thought of protesting—I did not want to see it, this portrait that was causing all the trouble. I did not want to confirm the nature of Catherine's relationship with him. I did not want to have to bear this burden. I still felt responsible, as I had introduced them, thinking that they could speak French together. I had no way of knowing what would happen, and yet I felt like an utter fool. How did it not occur to me that throwing these two sad, lonely souls together would result in disaster?

But it was my responsibility to see what I had done. Now someone was dead because of it, and Mr. Dryden—dear, dear Mr. Dryden—had put himself to a great deal of trouble and expense.

The back garden was a tangled mess. LaFrance clearly did not have a gardener, and the servants must have avoided going out there, as there were muddy puddles and a wild cat who leapt into our path from behind a shrub, then hissed and scampered away. Dead grass and weeds from summer were brown and trampled down in places. The shed was locked.

LaFrance let us in, and when I stepped inside, I was surprised to find the shed clean and dry. I looked up automatically, expecting to see a leaky roof, but it looked sturdier and better cared for than the main house.

"I would not leave my work in a damp shed," LaFrance said. "The light here is exquisite, and it is private."

"I do not know if I want to see the portrait," I said.

"You must," LaFrance replied.

"Stevenson will not be back," I told him. "You are safe. As is Catherine, if you will do the honorable thing and destroy it."

His brow wrinkled. "What happened to Stevenson?"

"He is dead."

There was a long pause. Then he let out a deep sigh. "I will not destroy it," he said quietly. "But I will keep it, just for myself."

"What if someone finds it?"

"I can protect it. It is the most valuable work I own. It shows me what I can really do and makes me excited for my future. And it is not finished. There is no reason why anyone should see it. I was a fool to show it to Stevenson—it was my ego. I will not make such a mistake again."

He turned and led me farther into the depths of the shed. I saw an easel set up in the back corner, where two banks of windows let in beautiful, filtered afternoon light. There was a sweet painting of a young girl clutching a doll propped up on the easel.

"My latest client," LaFrance said when he noticed me gazing at it. "I am doing quite well for work. I do not need to show anyone...this."

He pulled a large canvas out from a collection of canvases partly hidden under a gray drape.

I took a deep breath as he turned it to show me the painting.

I felt shocked dismay. It was Catherine; there was no doubt about it. And the pose, the way she was draped with a white sheet...I caught my breath and turned to LaFrance, gasping, "No one can see this."

"No one will see it," he said reassuringly. "It is for me."

I turned to stare at it once more. For this, I had killed a man. For this, I had inconvenienced Mr. Dryden. And this was going to seal my fate to Catherine's forever, there was no doubt. It would hang over both our heads for eternity.

It was also a work of genius. Even an untutored eye such as mine could see this. LaFrance might eventually become a famous and important painter if he could channel the emotion he clearly felt while painting Catherine.

"Can I not persuade you to destroy it?"

"Never," LaFrance said. "I want to remember her always. Just like this." He carefully returned the canvas to its place and pulled the gray fabric over it.

"It seems I must trust you," I said. I bit the words out. I do not trust anyone, as you well know, Booke! And the idea of trusting this skinny young Frenchman was appalling.

"If you love Catherine, you understand me," LaFrance said. "I love her as well. She is bold, exciting, powerful. I feel alive when I am with her. As do you, no? She inspires me to challenge myself."

He hesitated for a moment, then turned to me and gazed earnestly into my eyes. "But also, she trusted me. She trusts you. She has no choice. She is not free to live as she pleases, so she must trust the people in her life. True freedom is when you can live as you please and not trust anyone, anywhere. But is that desirable?"

I thought about this all the way home.

I am weary, dear Booke. I will not see LaFrance again, and God willing, neither will Catherine.

Am I free, dear Booke? Do I trust anyone?

I want to say that I do not. I trust YOU, of course. But people?

Everyone I have ever known has eventually abandoned me.

Does that mean I am free?

The only people who have not yet been brought to the test are Catherine and Mr. Dryden.

I do not think Catherine will abandon me. But it is true that when LaFrance tempted her, she succumbed. I think she has learned something of the world since then...but might she succumb again? Perhaps.

As for Mr. Dryden, I am perplexed. Why did he agree to help me when he would not accept my offer to marry him? He undertook risk in order to get us out of that terrible predicament with Mr. Stevenson, and I must trust him never to reveal the truth about what happened.

Does that mean I am not free?

I do not know the answer.

Your faithful friend,

Lydia

Chapter Thirty-Nine

MY TREASURED FRIEND,

It is very strange to be at Wansdyke again. The house and the servants are just as they were when we left. The bitterest cold of winter is behind us, and some days I feel a hint of moisture in the breeze, and it reminds me that snowdrops will soon appear.

Catherine is cheerful and chatty. I am amazed at her strength of spirit. On occasion, however, I see her staring hard out the window, her jaw set and her lips pressed firmly into a line as if she is holding herself together by sheer will.

Not a word from her father the earl, which is a relief.

There have been no letters from LaFrance. I have taken it upon myself to go through the post as soon as it arrives; the servants know that any communications are to be given to me directly. I can see that they are relieved that they do not have to speak to Catherine about subjects that usually provoke her temper. Anything having to do with her leg, they come to me and whisper, and I handle it myself. Their gratitude is why they have tacitly agreed to hand the management of the house over to me.

We have been to a few social events in Bath. However, I decline to sit with Catherine or to interact with the other guests. I am not a lady, I have decided. I am a servant—an upper servant to be sure, but a servant. I do not want any of the lying that comes with mingling in those circles. I think about my mama, the mistake she made with Papa, and the lies that were told in order to explain my existence. I have no use for any of it. I am content to have a roof over my head, and I need not engage in any of the false interactions that characterize society.

Sometimes I think about LaFrance's words about trust, that to be truly free is to trust no one.

Trust means vulnerability. We want to love, and we want to trust. But these are not always the best choices if we want to stay alive. I did not marry Mr. Dryden because I did not trust Lady Durand, and in that circumstance, my lack of trust kept me free of the risk that Mr. Dryden would harm me. And that lack of trust cost me Mr. Dryden, but perhaps that was a lesson I needed to learn.

I trust Catherine, and because of that, I accept that I am not free. She could harm me, I suppose.

But dear Booke, am I thus protected from the sad fate LaFrance spoke of—of becoming an embittered person who trusts no one in order to be truly free? I try to wake every morning with a smile, to exchange a friendly word with the maid who lights the fire in my room, to walk the meandering paths in the garden here at Wansdyke and wave at the gardener who prunes the shrubbery. I try not to be hardened or angry.

Is it enough?

For now, I believe it is. I do not need to be bitter. This is partly because I have you. I know you will always protect me and keep me strong. I have filled several pocket books with my thoughts and feelings, and by reflecting my own words back at me, you have always reminded me that I am strong and capable. As I near the end of this one, I feel compelled to thank you and to vow that our trust will never be broken.

It is time for me to start a fresh new book. I will see you there.

Ever your affectionate Lydia

Post script: Oh, Booke, I do not have any more room to write, so I will append this letter from Roman Dryden without explanation. My heart is pained. It is well that I will have no more interaction with the Durand family, as I do not think I could bear it. I am starting a fresh chapter in my life with Catherine. When I am able to write again, I will start a new pocket book, but right now, I think I need to rest my mind and my heart. I love you.

Chapter Forty

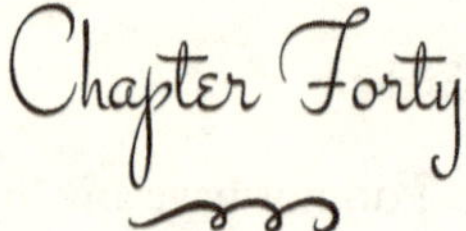

Letter from Roman Dryden

Harcourt House, Newark-on-Trent

To Miss Lydia Barrow

Wansdyke

Somerset

My dear Lydia,

I am aware that I have no right to be addressing you thus—please forgive me! This is the last letter you will receive from me, so I beg your indulgence. As I told you in London, you and your name are both beautiful, and I always think of you as Lydia. The sound of your name on my lips and in my mind gives me the strength to write to you one last time.

I have returned from London. My doctor assured me that the risk presented by travel was modest, as long as I was examined by my Yorkshire doctor promptly, which I was. All was well when I arrived back at Harcourt. I am blessed to have a devoted staff, many of whom are from families that have served mine for generations.

I do not know why I tell you this—forgive me. Perhaps it is because I regret very much that you will never meet these fine people. At one time...but never mind.

I find it difficult to get to the point of this letter, so let me begin by assuring you that the matter in London has been settled without fuss or fanfare. The case has been closed. The family of the person in question did not lodge any complaints or ask for redress of grievances. He was a bad person all the way round, and no one was surprised to hear that he had behaved so ill. A man who forces his way into a woman's residence after asking neighbors to make sure no one is home is not a man who will garner sympathy during an inquest. I regret that I was forced to state that you and I were engaged in a liaison, but I assure you that no one will hear of this lie aside from the few people who participated in the proceedings.

Now to my reason for writing.

I recently received a letter from your brother the viscount, making me aware that there has been some deception on the part of Lady Durand regarding the arrangements I made with your family. Therefore, I wish to tell you exactly what transpired.

The viscount said he understood that Lady Durand had paid me to marry you. Nothing could be further from the truth. In fact, my eyes must have started out of my head when I read those words. Paid me! As if I would have needed payment in order to be persuaded to make you my wife!

But even though I was not paid to make you an offer of marriage, I am still ashamed of my involvement in what was a heartless and cruel arrangement. I did not know you then, and I did not think of the morality of what I did, and for that I beg your forgiveness. But to be perfectly honest, I do not entirely regret what occurred, as the result was that I was able to meet you.

You will recall that I told you I could not renew my offer of marriage because I was promised to another. I beg your pardon for not being entirely candid. In fact, our families will very shortly be joined after all, because I am pledged to marry your sister Louisa.

I realize that this will come as a shock, and I am deeply sorry for not informing you of this development when we met in London, but I was filled with despair and regret and did not know what to say. My agreement with Lady Durand and the Duke could not be broken, so my heart was broken instead.

This is what transpired. After you declined my proposal, Lady Durand came to me, filled with apologies, and asked if I would consider marrying Louisa instead. I was quite surprised and not in favor. However, you had been clear in your refusal. What you did not know was that part of the agreement between your father and myself was the purchase of certain lands up north that I would use to expand my holdings. These were lands I desperately wanted, rich farmlands that abut my family's property.

I had approached the duke with an offer to purchase these lands a long time ago, as it appeared that they were very much neglected, but he sent my man of business away without hearing my offer. Last summer, however, I heard of some unfortunate new developments in the duke's affairs and made him another offer. After much discussion, he agreed to sell me the land, but the purchase was subject to a number of conditions.

Rather than being bribed to marry you, *I* paid the duke and duchess for the privilege of marrying you.

Yes, it is what it sounds like. I wanted the lands very much, but the price was unreasonable, so I made my own demand in return: I told them that I wanted a bride. And they gave me you.

I cannot tell you how it distresses me to write these words.

It is not unusual for marriage contracts to include some financial arrangement. But I wish to make a clean breast of this so you will know that my wish to marry you came from an honest place in my heart.

Your papa, you see, is deeply in debt, and nothing short of asking a ridiculous amount of money for the sale of properties he barely acknowledges would save him from public humiliation. I was able to purchase extensive tracts of land from him that will greatly extend my holdings around Nottingham and up into Sheffield, as well as secure my holdings in the Yorkshire area, where my family is from. If your father had sold his London townhouse, it would have caused gossip and speculation, but northern farmlands are of interest to no one in the society he values so much.

A few generations ago, we were poor sheep farmers. Now we are quite wealthy, and when I think about these new lands I have purchased from the Duke of Leicester, I feel great satisfaction. The reason, you see, is that on his deathbed, my father asked me to promise that I would not become a gentleman. You may think this odd, but please hear my story. My father was a farmer, like his father and his father's father, but he was also a wise man. I loved him very much. He raised me to love books and learning, but also to be proud of our Yorkshire heritage and our connection to the land he loved so much. He did not want me to become an educated gentleman with only a dim memory of where I was from, a foppish waste of the sacrifice and hard work of my family.

I was good at my books, however, so I channeled my brainpower into expanding our holdings and investing in the managers who have long served my family as caretakers. I have bankers in London, several men of business, and a large number of workers who live on my land and are devoted to my family. Indeed, I feel they are exten-sions of my family, and I take care of them with my father's admonition in mind that I not shame the many Dryden men who came before me.

However, the one thing I lacked was a bride, and there are complicated reasons for this. I have loved and lost, and I have become bitter. I have been unforgivably cynical about marriage and chose to engage only in dalliances that had no future. What follows is the unvarnished truth; I hope you will not despise me for it.

I am the father of an infant girl who will eventually be joining my household. She is currently in the care of a nurse in Yorkshire, but I do not wish her to grow up fatherless. Let us not speak of her mother, who cannot keep her. I no longer have any connection with her, and I fear for the child's safety and comfort, living as she does without either of her parents.

Thus, when Lord Durand's man of business came to speak to me about purchasing his northern properties at those outrageous prices, it occurred to me that perhaps the duke could take care of this problem as well. I never imagined that he would offer me his own daughter! I thought perhaps there was a gentlewoman in the family, perhaps a maiden aunt, who would like to mother a little girl.

The idea of a northerner like myself was very appealing. I did not say a word about the child, however. I merely stated that I was in search of a wife and that the deal would be conditional upon my acceptance of the candidate the family put forward.

During the negotiations, Lady Durand approached a mutual friend in London to offer you as my bride. It was a dark moment when I was distressed by certain other developments in my personal life, and did not hesitate to agree without asking any questions about you. I did not know Lady Durand, and I did not know that in offering you to me, she was engaging in an act of evil.

I am deeply ashamed—indeed, mortified—that I have been unable to bring myself to tell you the truth behind my sudden agreement to her offer of your hand. It was a stupid and arrogant arrangement indeed, as it treated you, a human being, as a commodity.

When I met you, I was speechless. I was also dismayed, because clearly it would be wrong to marry someone so young and beautiful when I am so much older and have much to apologize for in my life. But I was instantly head over ears in love, and I foolishly hoped beyond hope that you would have me, even though I was keeping this secret from you. Alas, you declined my offer, and I knew I deserved your refusal.

When you came to London, I thought perhaps the good Lord had given me a reprieve, that I might persuade you to have me after all. I also worried that you had heard tales about me from your family. They do not know about the child, but I knew they were displeased to have to grovel to one such as myself in order to save their family name. I was anxious to set things right, but unfortunately, we did not meet. And when Lady Durand offered Louisa in your place, I accepted because my heart was hurting and because I did not imagine that you would ever change your mind.

When we finally met and you told me you had changed your mind, I was devastated. If only I had waited! If only you had agreed to meet me sooner! But it was too late. The papers had been signed. I had sent a considerable sum to Lady Durand to be used for wedding clothes. Everything was in motion for an alliance between myself and your sister.

But when I heard the story of your childhood, I felt that God was showing me that my path was right. My daughter deserves the happy home you did not have. My heart was broken, but my purpose was firm.

My dear Lydia, I know not what else to say except that I am so sorry I was rash. Your loyalty and devotion to Lady Catherine and your strength of character are without rival. I know that having you by my side would have enriched my life.

It is my hope that you are not nearly as disappointed by this turn of events as I am. You made the choices that were best for you, and I understand. Nevertheless, I wanted to explain the connection between Louisa and myself, lest you interact with your family in the future and experience an unpleasant shock.

Louisa does not know about the child. I hope she will understand and forgive me for not telling her before our marriage and that she will love the child as she deserves.

I write this letter with much hope for your health and happiness. I promise not to disturb your peace again, but please know that you are in my heart forevermore.

I remain,

with devotion and regret,

your most ob'd,

Roman Dryden

Chapter Forty-One

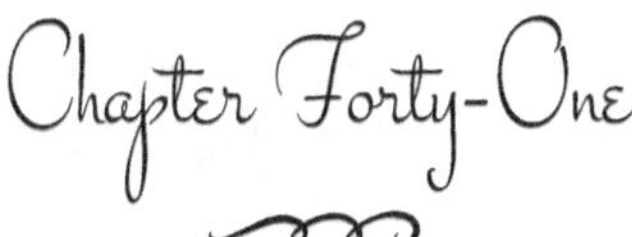

LETTER FROM DAVID LESLIE BUCKINGHAM DURAND, Viscount Howard

Merton College, Oxford

To Lydia Barrow, Wansdyke

Somerset

Lydia,

I have found him, and he knows to expect you.

Are you sure you want to do this? Do you need funds? I have not said a word to anyone, not even Marianne. If something should go wrong and you need help, you are to dispatch a letter to me through the Golden Goose. Everyone in Stroud knows it. Tell them to get it to me at Merton posthaste. I'll try to get to you as quickly as I can if I hear that you need me.

Lord, you're lucky one of my mates is the Earl of Gloucester. Otherwise I could not have put all of this together for you.

I still think you're mad, and I wish you weren't going through with it. There is really no need, and you know what is said about sleeping dogs, &c.

You're the best of my sisters, and I mean this heartily. Don't pay attention to Louisa or Mama. They need not get between us. And I will handle Papa, if he needs handling. Do what you must.

Yr most affectionate brother,

Howard

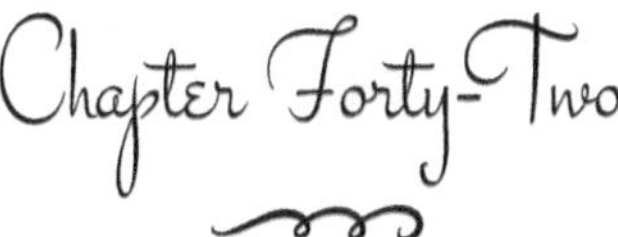

Chapter Forty-Two

My beloved Booke,

To start off a fresh new book with such a shocking letter from Mr. Dryden must have horrified you. It certainly horrified me.

When I received that letter, I was beside myself. All along, I thought Lady Durand had paid Mr. Dryden to get me out of Lydia's way and finally remove me from the family, but I was very much mistaken. Indeed, I was a fool, such a fool!

For apparently I was so inconsequential to the Durands that it was not necessary to go to such lengths. All along, I have fancied myself more important than I really was. How humiliating!

If I'd had any sense, I'd have realized that Lady Durand would never have spent money on me. It seems very obvious now. I have forever been a thorn in her side, even though I am not the one who hurt her. It was Papa, not me. But I am the one she has chosen to punish, because it is my existence that causes her pain, not Papa's crime.

It is quite ironic that in the end, I was able to help my family, not by agreeing to get out of the way but by being sold to Mr. Dryden. It's possible I was worth thousands of pounds, because Mr. Dryden would not have agreed to pay their price had they not provided a bride for him. By selling a daughter to Mr. Dryden, Papa can pay his debts and Lady Durand need not suffer humiliation in society.

I will not comment on what I think about Mr. Dryden purchasing a wife for himself.

All right, I WILL comment. I own that at first I was shocked and confused. I had thought he was in love with me. I even thought I might love him in return. I was willing to give up my commitment to Catherine to marry him, which I never would have done if I thought I could not love him.

But then I was angry. How DARE he. How dare he suppose that he could purchase a wife as simply as one might purchase a shawl or a pair of gloves? He thought there might be a "spare female" around Rosemont, I dare say? Someone who would not mind giving herself up to lifelong serfdom? Someone who would be willing to casually become the mother of a little baby, a minor indiscretion in the life of a wealthy man?

The bottom dropped out of my stomach when I realized he had bought me as a convenient solution to an inconvenient problem. And what's worse is that I still cannot rid myself of the desire that this should all be a great misunderstanding, that I should still be able to admire and respect Mr. Dryden as the one who saved Catherine from public shame and me from prison.

I still want so very much to fancy myself in love with him, just a little bit.

It was naught but a pleasant daydream, and this is the reality of life as a woman here on this planet. I am nothing but a commodity to be bought and owned, no matter how I feel about the purchaser.

I spent a few days at Wansdyke trying not to think about any of this. But I will admit, my mind kept returning to the child.

Louisa will be her stepmama! Louisa will be to her what Lady Durand was to me.

I tried to dismiss the thought, but I could not. Louisa still does not know that Mr. Dryden expects her to mother his little girl. This is quite a different outcome than Louisa expected when she journeyed to London for the Season. If I had been willing to marry Mr. Dryden, Louisa might have found happiness in some other union, but because I was not, Lady Durand had no choice but to offer him Louisa in my stead. And I know Louisa like I know my own mind. She is a cowardly, sad creature, and her faults manifest in cruel comments and vengeful behavior.

I feel ill that I bear responsibility for sentencing Mr. Dryden's innocent baby to a life of pain with Louisa as her mama. One day Louisa will doubtless do to her exactly what Lady Durand has done to me—remove her from the household, perhaps by selling her to some man somewhere, as she herself was sold.

I could not sleep for fretting over this.

So I made a decision. It may be a bad decision, or it may be a good one. And I will now explain about Master Howard's letter.

I have come to Gloucester to meet Mr. Jonathan Barrow.

I am sure you are wondering why! I am not sure how to reply, other than to say that I need to confirm for myself where I came from, who my mama's people are, and what favors Lady Durand did me when she plucked me out of my element.

I suppose I have not been very clear about my relationship to Mr. Barrow. We share a name, and that is it. Certainly Lady Durand never bothered to explain the particulars of my birth to me; everything I know comes from what I've gathered by eavesdropping. I've always understood that there was no need for the duke to acknowledge me, as Mr. Barrow had already done so. In fact, the duke's name not being listed on my birth record probably greatly improved Lady Durand's treatment of me. But beyond that, I know nothing.

I do not know where my mama is, so I cannot ask her any questions. But thanks to Howard (who it turns out is not a bad sort after all), I can ask Mr. Barrow instead.

I will not try to find my mama. I fear it will be impossible, and...

And...

I can only say this to YOU, dear Booke.

I am ashamed to admit it, but I am afraid of what I will find out. If she is not well, if she is deranged, if she is locked away somewhere, I am afraid to encounter her. I do not know how I will feel or how I will react. I fear I could not meet her even if I were to locate her. It seems absurd—I am now a single woman on my own, and I am afraid to risk an encounter with the woman who gave me life. But I need my peace of mind in order to move forward in this difficult world and to be supportive of Catherine.

In the hours before dawn, when it was very dark, on the day after I received Mr. Dryden's letter, I put on my shawl and went out to the gardens just beyond the drawing room. All was mist, as the ground was wet and the air was warm. It is not even Lent, but it feels as if winter has been over for a long time, with scarcely a sprinkle of snow. It was much colder at Rosemont.

I could not sleep. As I gazed out beyond the gardens, I asked myself whether I could do anything to help Mr. Dryden's little girl. She is the only one who is innocent in all of this. Mr. Dryden has done wrong, Lady Durand has done wrong, and if I do nothing, Louisa will do wrong.

I could see the answer clearly. I needed to find out if Lady Durand's decision to take me away from Jonathan Barrow was the right one.

All I know is my life as a duke's daughter. An illegitimate daughter, yes, but I was raised as a gentlewoman. I must see what my life would have been like if I had not been "saved" by Lady Durand. Everyone's circumstance is unique. But until I know more about my own situation, I will not know how I can help Mr. Dryden's child.

I am very weary, having been jostled and jolted on the road, and this inn Master Howard arranged for me is rather spare. I think he chose an establishment where his friend the earl could easily quiet any gossip, should things go wrong. It did not take long to get here, just a few hours, and it likely would have been faster if I had demanded it, but there was no need to hurry.

I ought not to be traveling without a maid, but for this errand I must be alone. I asked Catherine to trust me and promised to be back in a few days. As usual, her strength of character and utter confidence in her own mind amazed me. She looked me in the eye and said that I should use her carriage and groom and that she would ask no questions. I began to explain where I was going and why, but she held up a hand and said exactly what Master Howard said, which was to do what I must.

I will tell you all that transpires, dear Booke.

I am yours ever, ever, ever affectionately,

Lydia

Chapter Forty-Three

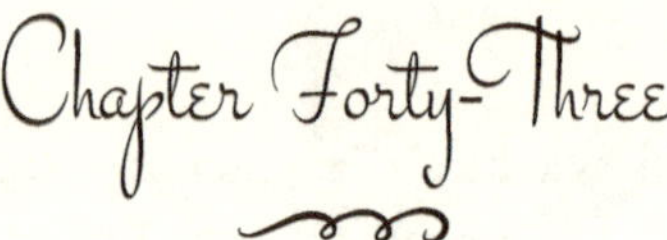

DEAREST BOOKE,

I write to you now in the almost-dark of an upstairs room at an inn at the edge of the market town of Stroud. Stroud itself is lively and fun. Bath is much nicer, of course, but Stroud is impressive for its size, its views, and its very steep streets.

But Stroud was not my destination. As I passed through it, I only looked out the window and wondered whether there were shops where I could sell my handkerchiefs and slippers—and there were! It has not occurred to me until then to branch out beyond Bath with my fine needlework, but in fact it would be quite doable! I could bring the items here myself, or I could hire someone to do it for me. I have so many ideas...

But let me get back to the most important thing I have to tell you. Because I have met Mr. Jonathan Barrow, the man who is legally my father. And after speaking with him, I also met my mother.

Yes, yes, I know—I swore I could not meet her. I did not want to encounter a crazy woman in a convalescent home. But let me tell you how it all transpired. It turns out I have been quite misled about my past and my people.

I admit I did not think about the fuss it would cause to drive into a village in an equipage like Catherine's. I grew up with carriages, so I thought nothing of it until I saw the looks on the faces of the villagers who came out onto the road to see what important person had decided to grace them with his presence.

I felt quite stupid. I should have come into the village in a cart or on a horse. Also, it did not occur to me to feel awkward in front of Barry the coachman and the undergroom he brought along, but they were probably mystified at my desire to visit a carpenter in a country town in the Cotswolds. Oh well.

I walked into Mr. Barrow's workshop and observed that it was very clean and well swept and smelled fragrantly of wood. There were two cats on a windowsill in the sun and a stove with a steaming kettle on it. When I entered, Mr. Barrow stood up slowly and nodded at me in a friendly way, then glanced out the window past the cats to where the carriage was waiting. When he saw it, his expression did not change, although his brow wrinkled slightly.

"Hello," I said, or tried to say. The word caught, and I had to cough and clear my throat before saying it again.

"Hello," he replied. "How may I help you?"

"My name is Lydia," I began, before remembering that it was Lady Durand who had insisted I be called by my middle name. "Actually, I am Lesley Lydia...Barrow," I said hesitantly.

Mr. Barrow's brow cleared. "Lesley!" He exclaimed. He came toward me, then stopped. It was then that I noticed he was old. Old as in grandfatherly. He was tall but slightly stooped and lean, but in an old-man wiry way. He did not shuffle, but he moved slowly.

"Is it possible? Is it really you? Why, you are quite grown up." He seemed shocked.

"It has been more than fifteen years," I said.

"They took you away," he murmured. He glanced out the window again, as if recollecting. "It was so sudden. Your poor mother." When he transferred his gaze back to me, his bright blue eyes had filled with tears. "Are you here to see her?"

At this point, I am quite sure I gasped loudly. I had never had the faintest intention of seeing my mother. As I said, I thought she was far away in a convalescent home; given that her "marriage" was not real, why would she be anywhere near Mr. Barrow? I thought it was all a sham.

"I am here to see you, Mr. Barrow," I said. I had practiced a speech all during the ride to the village, but it had flown out of my head, so I was forced to reach for words.

"That is kind of you," he said. He sniffled a little, took out a neat white handkerchief, and wiped his eyes. "You were a sweet little thing. I expect you must have many questions."

"I don't, actually," I said, surprising myself. "If the story I know is what really happened, I don't have any questions. I am just here to see you. To see—this." And I gestured around the workshop, toward the window. "I wanted to see where I am from."

"Your mother is a delightful lady," Mr. Barrow said. "She lives quite near here, and you should see her. It would lift her spirits." He sounded a bit sheepish as he added, "I spend my days and nights here in the workshop, but my sister visits with her daily."

I was shocked, then perplexed. Wasn't my mother insane? Suicidal? Far away in a home for the mentally unbalanced?

"I don't understand," I said. "I thought—" And then I realized that I couldn't say out loud what I had assumed, so I stopped. I needed to feel grown up and in control at all costs, as I am in charge of my own life now.

"Sit down, Miss Lesley," Mr. Barrow said. He was headed to the stove. "We'll have some tea."

"Let me get that," I said, but Mr. Barrow was already handling the kettle and a teapot and had found cups.

We sat and had tea, dear Booke. What a sweet, lovely man Jonathan Barrow is. It makes sense that someone like him would have offered to rescue my mother from her folly. He was a middle-aged bachelor, a builder and cabinetmaker of some repute, well off and alone. He did not know my mother well, but his sister had told him about her plight, and he was familiar with my mother's miniature portraits, which were famous in the area. He willingly stepped in to register himself as my father when I was born and never had cause to regret it, as he was very shy and did not have any interest in courting. He was already quite old when he and my mother married very quietly, and he eventually realized that I was his only heir, so he hoped I might come find him one day. When Master Howard's letter arrived, he was very happy and said he would welcome a visit.

I learned that my version of the facts was not completely wrong. But because of the way I learned those facts, whether by overhearing gossip or mean comments from Louisa, and because I was very isolated, there was important context that I did not understand. I did not know what it might be like to live in a small village amongst people who have known you and your family forever. I did not understand how that might be both a blessing and a curse.

According to Mr. Barrow, I was well cared for and much loved as a small child. His sister and my mother cared for me together. But it was true that the duke caused my mother grief and that she struggled with her mental health as a result. She had always been somewhat fragile and emotional, and after I was born, she became increasingly so.

The duke continued to visit her, and she grew ever more fretful, worrying that he would take me away from her if she broke things off with him or displeased him in any way. It was an open secret that the duke visited her, and Mr. Barrow did not try to prevent it. He was afraid of the duke's power and wealth, and he was also afraid my mother's fragile mind would collapse if he were to insist that she stop seeing him. He was my father in name only, so he was reluctant to intervene, even though the situation made for considerable discomfort in their community.

The story of Lady Durand removing me because of my mother's threats of self-harm was not quite right. Mr. Barrow told me that my mother threatened to harm herself BECAUSE Lady Durand removed me. She swept into the village one day and took me away, apparently furious that the duke had continued his relationship with my mother. Perhaps she thought that breaking up his "second family" would persuade him to stop visiting my mother.

I was in my nightgown, yes, because she literally took me from my bed, and when I wriggled out of her arms and escaped, crying, she ran down the lane to grab me and bundle me into the carriage. That is the origin of the nightgown story, which I had heard told in quite a different way.

The affair finally ended when I was taken away and my mama went out of her mind with the pain of losing her child. On the few occasions that the duke did try to visit, my mama ran to the bedroom window and tried to jump out. After that, he did not come again, and the villagers agreed that it was just as well that I was gone, given the shaky state of my mother's mind. This is how the twisted rumor began that I was taken away because my mother was on the verge of ending her life.

And the convalescent home? It was just Mr. Barrow's sister's home. My mother was so ill with grief over losing me that she had to be watched day and night. Whenever she saw Mr. Barrow, she would erupt into a fit of weeping and apologies, so she could not remain with him. My papa sent money to Mr. Barrow's sister for many years to support my mother, but these payments eventually stopped. Mr. Barrow supposed that Lady Durand had put an end to them. And with that, she managed to put an end to the duke's indiscretion.

I was aghast when I heard these stories. My mother was not insane? Or an unfit parent? Or locked away?

Mr. Barrow's eyes filled with tears once more as I asked him these questions. He shook his head. No. And no. And no.

But he did want to make one thing very clear. "It was better for you to live with the duke, my dear Lesley."

"I cannot see how!" I sputtered. "I should have been left here with people who loved me!"

"No," said Mr. Barrow. His voice was very gentle. "You are a lady now—look at you. And you are just as much your father's child as your mother's."

"I do not agree," I protested. "It was wrong of them to take me away."

"The manner of your leave-taking was abrupt," he agreed. "Lady Durand is quite a formidable woman. No one dared cross her. But you would have eventually suffered here. Life is not easy for your mother or for any young woman without protection. Your mother's family cut her off when she took up with the duke. She had nowhere to go and no one to help her but my sister and me. The people in the village would not speak to her. She could no longer sell her portraits. It was very difficult, and as you got older, it would have been even more difficult."

"I would have been a burden," I said. "Is that what you mean?"

"Never a burden," said Mr. Barrow. "But you would have been deprived of the benefits you were owed by your papa. It would have been unjust to keep you here, and your mother eventually understood that."

I wanted to ask him why he couldn't have protected me, why his kindness in giving me his name had not fixed every problem caused by my birth, but I was beginning to understand that even that kindness was no match for the harshness of the world. My feelings were all in a turmoil, dear one. Here I was with my legal papa, so kind and good, being told it was better that I live with my blood relations, as awful as they were. Was he right? I felt so strongly that he was wrong, but perhaps I simply did not know better?

He stood up, and I slowly rose to join him. I knew that he was taking me to see my mother, and oh, Booke, I was afraid! So afraid! That may seem strange, because I should have been eager. But I have spent my life thinking of my mother as a woman not in her right mind, someone Lady Durand needed to rescue me from. I simply could not square this new story with the image in my mind of a crazy person who endangered my life. I need my sanity right now more than ever, and I did not know how I would handle this encounter.

We walked around the corner and down a lane, past other tidy cottages made of honey-colored Cotswold stone. The cloudy sky threatened rain, and a stiff breeze was blowing. A stone wall ran alongside the lane, which was dry and clean. I must admit that I had not imagined such a lovely setting for the home of my supposedly deranged mother.

Mr. Barrow called out to her from the front walk when we arrived. When she emerged from the house, I was startled, as I think I had expected her to look like me, and she did not at all! I resemble the duke, and my mother is practically the opposite. Where the duke is tall, she is short. Where he is dark haired and strong featured, she is pale and fair with straw-colored hair swept into a bun that was coming loose at her neck.

She looked very young, much younger than Lady Durand. I was horrified that perhaps the duke had taken advantage of a mere child—she looked not much older than myself. But that could not be, I realized, doing the sum in my head. She simply looked very young, perhaps because of her paint-stained apron and the smudges on her cheeks.

She recognized me instantly and froze.

"Lesley," she said. "It is you, isn't it?"

Mr. Barrow did not let me answer. He seemed concerned that my mother would be upset and perhaps even swoon. He hurried to her and took her hand.

"Rosie, dear, look who has come to see you."

"I know who it is," she said. "It's Lesley. Is—is—" She peered up the lane from whence we'd come.

"I am alone," I said.

"Did he tell you I was here?"

I shook my head, feeling awkward. I did not know what she wanted to hear, so I was afraid to speak.

Her face fell. Then she smiled. "I am happy you came to see me."

"I did not know you lived here," I said. "I thought you were—" I stopped, not knowing how to explain that I'd thought she was insane and living behind locked doors.

There was a long pause, and her eyes searched my face, looking for answers. I wondered what she hoped to find.

"Are you well?" she asked finally.

"Yes."

"The family—they treat you well?"

I wasn't prepared for that question! Very stupid of me, Booke, I know. Did I tell her the truth, that I had been cast out? Did I lie? Did I make up a story?

Mr. Barrow rescued me. He stated firmly that I had come into the village in a fancy carriage, and didn't I look well enough?

My mother nodded shyly, taking in my new dress and hat, which I had chosen especially for the day. I had not wanted to arrive on Mr. Barrow's doorstep looking needy or desperate, after all.

"I just wanted to see you," I said to her suddenly. I don't know what prompted me to spit out that sentence, but it was the honest truth. I did not have an agenda or a plan; I had not even known I would see her. I just wanted to see this world I had come from, to match it against the world I knew. I wanted to meet the people who were important to me long before I could remember, people I had forgotten.

I wanted to consider in an informed way whether Mr. Dryden should bring his little girl into his home to be parented by Louisa. Was that the right choice?

I wanted to weigh Lady Durand's half truths against the facts these people had. Lady Durand had not lied completely, but she had massaged the truth to suit her purposes. I'm sure everyone does this in order to make ourselves believe that we are not bad people. We do what we do, and then we explain, and in the course of explaining, we massage. I think this is just how humans survive. But Lady Durand caused so much harm with her lies, deception, and manipulation. I wanted to know what the alternative might be.

"I've wanted to see you also," my mother said. She approached me slowly, wiping her hands on her apron. "I have paint on my hands," she said in apology. Then she extended her hands to take mine. I felt the grit of the paint on her palms and her fingertips and smelled the strong chemical scent of solvent.

"You still paint?" I asked.

She nodded.

"She is well known throughout the area and beyond," Mr. Barrow said proudly.

"That is how you met him," I said, and then regretted it as my mother's hands stiffened.

But she nodded and replied, "Yes." She looked fondly about the yard. "He bought this house for us, but I was not well after you were born. I lay abed most days. He would come and visit me sometimes. You used to run around here in the yard, and Jonathan would chase you—"

Mr. Barrow chuckled. "I remember that! You were a fast one," he said to me.

My eyes traveled up to the second level, where there was a window framed by white curtains. Was that the window she had threatened to throw herself out of? Or was that just another half truth designed to make Lady Durand look virtuous?

"I was not well," my mother said again. I looked back at her, wondering if she knew why I was looking at the second-story window.

"When did you last see him?" I asked. I suddenly wanted to know. How much had Papa loved my mama? How long was it before he tired of her, before my mama's crazed grief and threats of self-harm made him give her up?

I had always reasoned that he must have abandoned her quickly. Men were like that, I thought—they toyed with women and then tossed them aside. If he had really loved my mama, he would have treated me better. He would have gotten to know me. He would have paid attention. Perhaps my assumptions were simplistic, but I knew nothing of men or affairs of the heart, if that was indeed what had happened between my mama and the duke.

My mother did not reply, however. She was smiling at me, squeezing my hands between her paint-stained fingers.

"You have become such a fine lady," she whispered.

"Please," I begged. "When did you last see Papa?"

My mother was still smiling. "I loved him very much, my dear. So in the end, I sent him away and begged him not to return. And while I was upset with Lady Durand for taking you from me, I see now that it was the right thing to do. You are so beautiful, such a fine lady." Her smile was trembling, and the pressure of her hands was strong, gripping my fingers so tightly that it hurt.

So they had loved each other. I could feel it in her hands and see it in her eyes.

I almost wished this were not so. Life is so cruel.

But my mother was strong and independent. She could have remained the duke's mistress, but she chose to go it alone.

There were tears in my eyes and in hers as she let my hands go.

"Wait here," she said, and went back into the house. A moment later, she returned with something in her hands. It was a white handkerchief with an elaborately embroidered pheasant set at a diagonal in one corner, the initials RLR buried in its tail.

"These are my initials," she said. "I dare say you do not know my full name. It is Rosemary Lydia Robinson." She gave it to me, and I found that it was wrapped around something small and hard.

It was a miniature of a laughing girl with dark curls.

Me.

"You should not give this to me," I protested. "You should keep it."

"I give this to you that you may someday give it to someone who deserves it, someone who loves you," she said. She leaned forward to kiss me.

"I embroider handkerchiefs, too," I said through my tears. She laughed and wiped my cheeks with her thumb.

"Do not cry. All is well."

"I will return someday," I promised. "I need...time."

She stepped back and nodded. "I understand."

Booke, I could have stayed all day. I could have stayed for many days. But my story, which began in that house, is no longer in that house.

My story is at Rosemont.

My story is with Papa, Lady Durand, Howard, Louisa, and Marianne. And now Catherine.

It is a painful story, sometimes a sad story. But it's my story, and I am owed a truthful version of it, so I took it back into my own hands.

I'm very glad that I was able to untangle it.

One last thing about Mr. Barrow. He told me as we walked back to his workshop that as I am his only legal heir, I will inherit everything he has. He seemed content to tell me this. He also asked if all was well with my life at Rosemont, and I lied and told him it was. No need to worry him, after all. As he handed me up into the carriage, he leaned forward and said, "I have a lovely young lady for a daughter."

By the time I turned to reply, he had stepped back and was nodding to the coachman. We set off, and he waved at me, his smile creasing his eyes so that I could just barely make out his tears.

I must visit again soon.

Yours ever affectionately,

Lesley Lydia Barrow

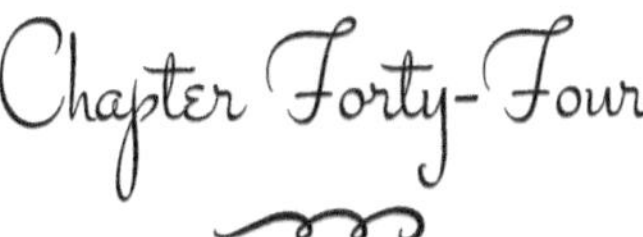

Chapter Forty-Four

My dearest Booke,

I have returned to Wansdyke. When I stepped out of the carriage, I was astonished that nothing had changed, for I felt that I had grown so much older. I even checked my reflection in a mirror as I washed the road grime from my face and neck, thinking that surely I must have aged while I was away!

Catherine squealed like a child when she came into the drawing room and found me. I do love her so!

While I was on the road, I mentally composed a letter. Can you guess to whom? No?

I am teasing you.

No, it is not to Mr. Dryden. I am done with lies and half truths. I am also done with apologies for lies and half truths.

It is a letter to Louisa.

I know I do not need to tell you what I said. But there were no lies or half truths in it.

I am so tired now, dear Booke. I must rest.

Yours ever so affectionately,

Lydia

Chapter Forty-Five

LETTER FROM MARIANNE DURAND

Rosemont

OH, my dear Lydia!

We are in an uproar. Everyone keeps things from me, so I do not know all. I wish I could tell you exactly what has happened, but the more questions I ask, the more violently I am dismissed. Neither Mama nor Louisa will explain, but Louisa is in her room all day every day, sobbing. She has made herself ill with crying, and Mama has been quite unlike herself, shouting at Louisa that she is a lucky girl and must stop sulking.

It has something to do with that awful man Mama tried to have you marry, the one you refused. You were wise to do so. Howard and I both thought he had a dirty secret, and I believe this is proof that he was never the man Mama thought he was. She was deceived, alas. While in London, he offered for Louisa, and Louisa accepted. Why, I do not know, as I only heard about this after Louisa came home, but I imagine it had something to do with the lands he had purchased. I asked, but no one would tell me.

But within a few days of arriving home, Louisa received a letter. It was at the breakfast table, and as soon as she read it, she gave a great cry and fell into a swoon. She has been sobbing ever since and will not eat or drink.

All I can puzzle out is that Louisa was willing to marry him in London but has discovered something about him that has changed her mind, and Mama will not allow her to break the engagement.

What do you know about that man, Roman Dryden? Do you know what could have made Louisa so ill? I am very worried about her. I am perplexed that she ever wanted to marry a farmer, and even more perplexed that Mama is forcing this marriage on her.

Right now, Louisa is screaming that she would sooner throw herself into the river than marry him, and Mama is screaming back that she is an ungrateful child. The servants are whispering and Papa is nowhere to be found.

I am frightened, dearest Lydia. Is there any light that you can shed upon this? You were in London very recently, and I gather you must have seen Louisa and Mama there. Have you met this Roman Dryden?

Howard is not here, and I have no one to talk to. I await your reply.

Yrs with much love,

Marianne

Chapter Forty-Six

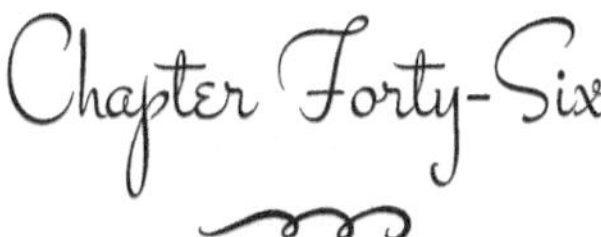

BELOVED FRIEND,

I have caused an uproar at Rosemont, it seems. I would laugh if the situation were not so grave.

With a stroke of my pen—all right, I am being overly dramatic, not with a *single* stroke of my pen, but with my letter to Louisa—I have broken Mr. Dryden's contract with my papa.

I told Louisa that Mr. Dryden had a child.

I told her that this is why Mr. Dryden offered for her, in case she thought it was for her beauty or status. He needs a mother for his child.

I also told Louisa that he had written to me about the child, in case she wanted to dispute me. I invited her to ask her mama for the truth.

I have not heard from Louisa, but that is no surprise. However, I heard from Marianne. I slipped her letter into these pages. After the dust has settled, I will write to her to explain, though it grieves me very much to have to tell her that Lady Durand was ready to sell Louisa just as easily as she was ready to sell me.

When I received Marianne's letter, I was sitting in the drawing room with Catherine. I think she must have realized immediately that it was news from Rosemont. She begged me to tell her all, and I was casting about, trying to think of how I should begin, when believe it or, Mr. Dryden was announced.

Mr. Dryden!

Yes, Mr. Dryden is here. He did not even send a note but simply showed up, exhausted and worn from hard travel. He apparently drove at top speed to get here as quickly as possible, all the way from his home in Newark-on-Trent.

He charged into the drawing room, begging our pardon for his sudden arrival but looking so white and drawn that we both exclaimed in horror. Catherine shouted for a manservant to take him to the nearest bedroom and help him wash, as he has come without a valet or servant. He refused to leave, however, stating that he would say what he came to say.

At this, Catherine excused herself, and I was left alone with Mr. Dryden.

I wondered what on earth was he doing here. He looked very ill, dear Booke! His complexion was sallow, and he seemed to have lost weight. He had been very thin when I last saw him, and now he was thinner still. He was still dressed in brown and wore dusty brown boots and a dusty brown hat, which he had removed and was crushing in his hands.

As I stared, I remembered how angry I had been, how hurt I had been, when I'd received his letter. Was he thinking that an apology would suffice?

"You did not have to come all this way, Mr. Dryden," I said as coldly as I could. "I received your letter, in which you explained yourself quite well. It must have been a terrible journey. Did you come from Nottingham?"

"I did," he said. "But I paid a visit to Rosemont on the way, so it was not quite as long a journey."

Rosemont? Ah, yes. Of course. There was an uproar at Rosemont, one that I had caused. Doubtless he had gone there to try to save his land purchase. And his bride purchase.

I tried not to let the bitterness show on my face, but it was hard, dear Booke. The pain of my visit to my mother was fresh, and the realization that no matter how difficult my life at Rosemont had been, it was my life, the only one I had, and also the life that I should have had, for I was a Durand, too. After all, Louisa was to be my replacement as Mr. Dryden's wife because we were interchangeable Durand daughters, apparently.

"I am here to apologize to you in person," Mr. Dryden said anxiously. There were two spots of color high on his cheeks. Concerned, I interrupted to say I thought he should sit down. A knock at the door announced the arrival of a tea tray, and I took a moment to dismiss the maidservant and pour the tea.

"Mr. Dryden," I said, "you must have this cup of tea before you speak further. I insist. You are unwell."

"I am not unwell!" he cried. "I am merely desperate! I have done a great wrong to you, Lydia. Will you forgive me?"

"I am a Christian," I said, "so I have already forgiven you. Let us consider the subject closed."

"No," he said. "You are angry. And you have every right to be angry. But you are not letting me make amends. I love you, dear Lydia."

When I heard the words, something twisted in my heart, for I knew it was true. Even though I was furious, offended to my very core, I believed that Mr. Dryden had traveled a great distance to see me because he loved me. He had made a very bad mistake, and he had come to fix it. What more honorable gesture could there be?

But I was also still angry, hurt, and full of so many other emotions, I could not think straight. It was as if there was a thick, foggy haze surrounding me.

At this point, overwhelmed, I sank down into a chair. I did not cry, but I was exhausted beyond feeling. I had spent too many hours thinking about Rosemont, Lady Durand, Mr. Barrow, and my mother, and I was worn out.

Mr. Dryden sat beside me and took my hands, and I tried to pull them away, but Booke, I did not fight very hard! His hands were warm, almost hot, and mine were cold. He pressed them to his lips briefly before replying.

"When Louisa heard about the child, she went into hysterics. And of course, by then I knew that I could not let someone like Louisa mother my child. And besides, I loved you. Your loyalty to Lady Catherine, your strong character...I knew I could not marry anyone else. I thought I could not break my engagement, that it would not be honorable—all the contracts had been signed, and everything was fixed—but I realized that it would be worse to marry her while I still loved another. I did not have to break the engagement, however, because Louisa broke it for me."

"Of course she did," I said bitterly. "She would never have entered into such a situation willingly. It would have been a repeat of her mother's experience. I am surprised that Lady Durand did not force her to accept it, however."

"She might have," Mr. Dryden replied. "But I told her that I would not have an unwilling bride."

At this, I turned away, feeling ill. Mr. Dryden knew what I was not saying—that I was revolted by the reminder that he had paid the Durands for a bride.

"I beg your forgiveness," he said. "I decided I would pay only a fair price for the land to show that I was not ascribing a price to Louisa or to you. I do not want to put a price tag on a mother for my daughter. It was wrong of me from the start, but I was in a panic over how to do right by the child. My first thought was that I must not abandon her. She does not even have my name, as I was not married to her mother when she was born."

"But what of her mother?"

He shook his head. "She is a good-hearted, friendly soul, the daughter of an innkeeper. I stayed at this inn frequently when inspecting my properties in Yorkshire. Her mother is dead, and she had no one to look out for her. She was lonely and good company. But I have served her a very ill turn indeed. When she discovered that she would have a child, I paid for her to travel far away and have the baby in secret so as not ruin her life. As miserable as this made her, it was the only way to avoid serious consequences to her ability to run her father's tavern. She was fortunate that her father did not throw her out; he needs her help and cannot afford to lose her, so he reluctantly agreed to my scheme to spirit her away until the baby was born."

"Do you not want to marry her?"

"I do not," Mr. Dryden said heavily. "And she does not want to marry, either. She does not love me; she has made this clear. She will inherit the tavern from her father, and she wishes to remain where she is. Anyone she marries must be willing to take over the tavern, which I am not." He smiled a little, wryly. "She is strong and independent, like you."

"But do you love her?"

"I do not," Mr. Dryden said again. "She has much to recommend her, but I do not love her. We were merely two lonely souls. And as painful as it was for her to give up the girl, she did not want a child. I promised her that I would do right by the baby, but because she does not have my name, the most I can do is to raise her well. Though she will not legally inherit my properties, I will fund a generous trust for her so that she will never know privation. But a girl needs a mother, and I thought I could acquire one for her by asking the duke and duchess to help me. Unfortunately, it has all gone wrong."

At this point, dear Booke, Mr. Dryden seemed to be on the verge of a faint. I rose and helped him up as best as I could, settling him into the chair nearest the fire, and made him drink the rest of his now-cooled cup of tea. Now that he had told me what he had come to say, the feverish tinge had left his cheeks, and he seemed spent but more in control of himself. After a few moments, Catherine came in to say that a room had been prepared for him and that a servant would escort him upstairs so he could rest a few hours before dinner.

Can you believe it, dear Booke? Mr. Dryden is in a room down the hall. Life is so very strange.

You are the best of friends!

Lydia

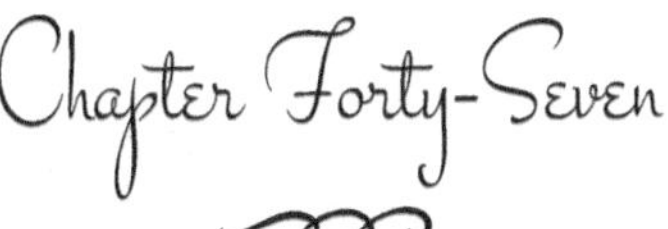

Chapter Forty-Seven

DEAREST BOOKE,

I have thought hard about what I want.

So much has happened since I was trying to sell handkerchiefs and slippers in Bath.

I am no longer a part of the Durand family.

I have a trusted friend, a position in her household, and her support as I continue to work on my business.

I have learned the truth about my "rescue" from Mr. Barrow.

I have met my mother.

And I have been loved by a man.

If things had been different—indeed, if the events of the past six months had played out in a different order—I might have loved Mr. Dryden in return. Indeed, I do love him. But I will not marry him.

I was very, very close to wanting to be married, just to end the stressful journey of trying to be my own person, an independent woman, which is not an easy thing. But I have Catherine instead of a man to be my lifelong companion.

Choices are tricky. So much depends on the order in which events happen. I was wandering the lane in my nightgown when Lady Durand swooped down to grab me and take me to Rosemont, but only because I had run away from her in the first place, not because my mother had neglected me.

The order in which things happen matters a great deal.

With his burden of guilt lifted, Mr. Dryden was in better spirits at dinner. He praised Wansdyke, asked after Catherine's health, and offered advice on the care of the barley fields that I had no idea even existed. Catherine is completely uninterested in barley fields but tried very hard to keep a straight face and mostly succeeded.

By the end of dinner, it was clear that Catherine had mostly forgiven Mr. Dryden for trying to take me away from her. She mostly forgave him for being a man in love, in other words. She also told him how deeply grateful she was that he had rescued her from her folly in London; she has very pretty manners when she chooses, and I was impressed at her willingness to be humble.

Mr. Dryden tried to dismiss her thanks, saying bluntly that in some matters, only a man of means is able to cut through a sticky mess, and that he was glad to be of service. He also said a bit sternly (as of course he is much older than Catherine, old enough to be her father) that he hoped she would not have any future dealings with LaFrance and his comrades. I thought she would bristle at his paternal tone, but she was suitably contrite.

Mr. Dryden retired early, and Catherine and I were left sitting in front of the fire with our tea.

"You should marry him," she said to me suddenly as I stood to fuss with the teapot.

"I am not marrying anyone," I replied.

"He is so in love with you," she continued, but I shrugged and returned to my seat without replying.

"I feel as if I am reading a romance novel," Catherine said. "And while I do not want you to leave my side, I almost feel as if I would not be turning the pages if I did not say the obvious. If you do not marry him, the story will not conclude properly."

"But I have a story, too," I protested. "And so do you. I do not want to be a detail in a man's life."

"Ah. Yes, you are right. That is what we have been. It is better to star in our own stories."

There was a pause, after which Catherine added wistfully, "But a love story with a happy ending is so nice."

"A friendship story with a happy ending is also nice," I said.

"Do you not feel the least bit of regret?"

"Not at all," I said, but I was not telling the truth. Dear Booke, I felt a huge amount of regret. But I will not tell Catherine this. As much as I value the truth, I value our friendship even more. And I do not want Catherine to think that she is depriving me of happiness, or indeed that the only stories that matter are those that end in marriage.

I changed the subject and told her about the shops I had seen on the High Street in Stroud and how I thought I could sell my slippers and handkerchiefs there, at which Catherine complained that I should not need to make so much money. But when I pointed out that her father still had some control over her purse, even though Wansdyke is her property through her dead mother, she grew grave and said she was lucky to have me, as she had no one else to teach her these things.

I think I have made a good choice to invest in myself and my friendship with Catherine.

If only my heart did not skip a beat whenever I think of Mr. Dryden.

What do you think, dearest Booke? I tell you things I do not even tell Catherine. You alone know what is in my heart, the hopes and dreams I bury deep down.

Am I foolish to give up on love?

But perhaps I am not giving up on love. Perhaps I simply do not want that kind of love—right now, at any rate.

It is late, and I have had quite the day, dear Booke. I give you a kiss and a salute, for you are always here for me.

Much love to you, and very affectionately yours,

Lydia

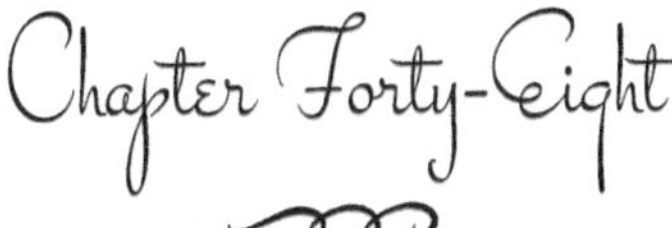

Chapter Forty-eight

Dearest one,

It seems that even if I have given up on love, it has not given up on me.

Funny how it takes two people to love. One-sided love isn't really love, but two people who love each other can create an explosion that expands outward and affects those around them.

Mr. Dryden left today. But before he left, he told me once again that he loved me. Would I marry him?

I believe he knew the answer. He has seen me with Catherine and knows I will not leave her.

But this time, I was sure he was asking me for myself, not because he needed me to do menial tasks in his home and parent his unfortunate little girl.

Catherine had left us alone after breakfast on the pretense of scolding the kitchen staff. The room was empty but for us. Mr. Dryden came up to where I sat and without hesitation knelt to ask me if I would marry him.

I reached out to touch his cheeks, roughened by years of weather and neglect, and smoothed the messy brown hair from his brow, privately thinking that he needed something better than the black riband that only somewhat managed to keep it pulled back at his neck.

"You have made me fall in love with you, despite everything," I said.

I admit that my lip trembled as I said this. Perhaps I should not have said it. But I am so tired of lies, and the heart feels what it feels.

"I do not deserve it," he said.

"No," I agreed, "but we all do foolish things on occasion. I'm sure Lady Durand could tell you about many of my childhood antics. I am not immune to error."

He was silent for a moment, then grasped my hands and pressed them to his heart.

"But I need to carry through on my promises to Catherine and to myself," I said. "I must always able to take care of myself, and I want to help Catherine do the same. She is a child, you know."

"I will wait for you."

"Will you?"

"Yes," he said firmly.

"I do not know if I will ever be ready to marry you. Marriage is not like...like hiring a servant, you know. Or it should not be, anyway."

"I will wait."

"You will wait at your own risk," I said. "I do not promise anything. I am devoted to Catherine."

He was silent. For a long moment, he held both my hands, pressing them against his heart. I could feel it beating beneath his shirt, light and quick. It occurred to me that a big man like Mr. Dryden, someone who is often outdoors on his land, should not have a light, quick pulse.

"Are you ill, Mr. Dryden?" I asked suddenly. I was thinking of the London doctor visits, his occasional mentions of being unwell, his sallow complexion and very thin frame. "You have gotten thinner. And you seem—"

"So I have been found out," he said lightly.

With that, he released my hands, and I felt a jolt of panic. Was he dying? Is that why he was so worried about his little girl?

"What is wrong?" I asked. "You said you saw doctors in London. You said you—"

"I am not dying," he said. "But I was recently very ill and went through a long period of convalescence. The doctors say that as long as I do not tax myself, I will live many more years. I cannot work outside among my people anymore and must devote myself to my books. Believe me, it does not distress me to receive this news! I like being indoors in my library. And I have a new appreciation for living. But this is why I feel I must provide well for my daughter. Life is precious."

"Did you suffer permanent harm from your illness?" I asked.

Mr. Dryden shrugged. "Perhaps, perhaps not. I am frequently tired, and I sometimes find myself gazing into space. But perhaps this is not a physical illness. Perhaps it is melancholy. Perhaps it just means that I must live right and do right in order to feel right."

"Have you...have you canceled your land purchase?"

I desperately wanted to know. Louisa had not replied to my letter, of course, and I didn't think Marianne would know anything about a land purchase. I was hoping to avoid writing a letter to Howard about all this.

"No," he said. "No, I am going ahead with it. It is important to me. My father would have wanted this. Of course, I am not going to pay what the duke demanded."

"Well, that price included one of his daughters." I tried not to sound bitter. "That would not be right."

He nodded. "They have agreed to a much fairer price. Without the inclusion of a daughter." He smiled wryly.

"Can you bring your little girl to your home even without a wife?" I dreaded his answer, for I had seen the home I had been ripped away from. I wished so much that I had been left with Jonathan Barrow and my mother, but I had to confess that Rosemont was the evil I knew versus the evil I did not know. My mother and Jonathan Barrow were so sure that being brought up as a lady with the Durand children was more beneficial to my future than being the village outcast's daughter.

"I just want to do what is right," he said quietly. "I will bring her to my home, and her nurse will come with her. Even without a mother, she will be loved. I will take care of her. I will offer her everything I can."

"What is her name?"

"Gillian. Gillian Mary Dryden."

"Gillian Mary Dryden. That is a beautiful name."

"She was given her mother's name at birth, as we were not married. But I will insist that she be addressed by my name."

I took from my pocket the handkerchief my mother had given me. It has become very precious to me, as you know, dear Booke. I keep it with me always, and I take it out many times a day to study it. I marvel at her perfect little stitches, the glowing colors of the pheasant that melt into each other and create a shimmer on its breast. Perhaps her talent as a painter is what helps her to blend the colored threads so expertly. I have resolved to become better at drawing and painting; perhaps it will help the sales of my needlework!

Today I had my mother's miniature with me in my pocket. I unwrapped the handkerchief and gave the tiny portrait to Mr. Dryden, who exclaimed and held it up for closer inspection in the morning light.

"Why, it is you!"

"Not quite," I corrected. "It is my mother's imagination of me. She did not know what I would grow up to look like. She painted this based solely on what I looked like as a small child."

"But it is nearly perfect!" He held it up next to my face.

"It is," I agreed. He put it back in my palm, and I tucked it away into the handkerchief again. What I did not say was that my mother had given it to me with the heartfelt wish that I would give it to someone who loves me. And I realize now that the person who loves me is...me.

This portrait is mine.

Then I said to him, "I am sorry for everything. I hope you will not forget me."

"I will not forget you," Mr. Dryden exclaimed. "I will wait for you. I promise I will."

"Do not wait for me," I said. "But after enough time has passed, I will visit Rosemont again, and when I do, I will visit you, too. And perhaps I will meet your little girl."

"I hope so," Mr. Dryden said.

He has left, and I am a little sad, but mostly content.

I will make my own way in the world.

I will help Catherine to make her way.

I may eventually marry, but only as I please, when I please, whom I please.

I believe this is trust tempered with prudence, which is the best way forward.

Ever your affectionate,

Lesley Lydia Barrow

Special Offer

FOR READERS OF EVER YOUR AFFECTIONATE

I hope you enjoyed this book!

Ever Your Affectionate is the prequel to my novel, *The Portrait*. Where *Ever Your Affectionate* is about Lydia, *The Portrait* is about Catherine.

I love romantic stories, but I don't love bad historical detail, and I don't love stories where the female characters are wilting, fragile victims of their lives. When I couldn't find stories that sounded brave and authentic (yet honestly vulnerable), I decided to write my own. I don't know if I've met my own standards, but I'll keep writing until I do.

You can grab a special ten-chapter giant chunk of *The Portrait* by going to mayarushingwalker.net/portraitsample, if you're interested in more of Catherine's story. Or get my contemporary novella *Ghost of Tomorrow*, the prequel to my novel, *Coming Home to Greenleigh*, by signing up for my newsletter via my website, mayarushingwalker.net.

You can unsubscribe from the newsletter any time, but I often hand out my books for free to my newsletter friends, so it may be worth it to stick around!

Acknowledgments

The book is finally done, midwifed by editor extraordinaire Allison Cherry. Thank you for redirecting me whenever my muse tried to take the wrong exit.

Thank you to the other residents of this old farmhouse, where we hunkered down together and survived the events of the past year.

Nora K., you are always my chief cheerleader. You make all the difference for me.

And thank you to all the readers of *The Portrait*, especially those who wrote to me and begged to hear Lydia's story. Thank you for your patience and your persistence. Catherine isn't done with me yet!

About the Author

Maya Rushing Walker writes contemporary and historical fiction. She lives and writes in a 1780s farmhouse in northern New England. This is her fifth book.

Find her books online at mayarushingwalker.net.

Also by Maya Rushing Walker

The Portrait

Coming Home to Greenleigh

Ghost of Tomorrow

Frankenstein by Mary Shelley: A Story Grid Masterworks Analysis Guide